OUT OF
TEMPT...

BY
VALERIE PARV

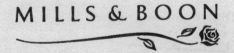

MILLS & BOON

MILLS & BOON LIMITED
ETON HOUSE, 18-24 PARADISE ROAD
RICHMOND, SURREY TW9 1SR

*First published in Great Britain 1994
by Mills & Boon Limited*

© Valerie Parv 1994

*Australian copyright 1994
Philippine copyright 1994
This edition 1994*

ISBN 0 263 78506 8

*Set in Times Roman 11 on 12 pt.
01-9406-48320 C*

Made and printed in Great Britain

CHAPTER ONE

JILL RICHTER smoothed a hand over the tawny head of the orphaned calf as it drank greedily from a baby's bottle. She had to hold the bottle tightly to prevent it from being tugged out of her hand with each intake of milk.

'This one can't have eaten for a week,' she told Denise, who watched, arms folded across the bulge of her advanced pregnancy.

Her sister-in-law grinned back. 'More like since this morning. He's a con artist, that one. Don't give him more than his fair share.'

'Easier said than done.' The calf had already drained one of the banana-shaped bottles. Jill hadn't the heart to deny him a second helping, although Denise was probably right. As she concentrated, Jill's dark hair cascaded past her shoulders, curtaining her classical features. Under the deep brow, her teal-blue eyes shone with enjoyment.

'Gets to you, doesn't it?' Denise observed.

Not entirely truthfully, Jill shook her head. 'Not a chance. Sorry, little one, you've had your lot.'

She took the bottle away from the lowing calf who craned his satiny neck to follow it, only giving up when Jill retreated outside the paddock.

Denise gave her a knowing look. 'So you still say motherhood isn't for you?'

Jill nodded in the direction of Denise's bulge. 'Given the state of my love-life, it seems unlikely. I'll have to settle for aunthood, won't I?'

Denise sighed. 'Pity. It would have been fun to have someone share the experience with me.'

'Aren't you forgetting one small detail?'

'You mean the fact that you don't have a husband? I don't see why it matters when they contribute about three minutes to the whole nine-month performance.'

Wiping her hands on the sides of her figure-hugging jeans, Jill laughed. 'You'd better not let Nick hear you dismiss his contribution so lightly. This baby is already the apple of his eye.'

Her sister-in-law's eyes clouded. 'I know. It means so much to both of us. What if it turns out like the last time?'

The hand which gripped Jill's arm was deathly tight, and Jill patted it reassuringly. 'You know the doctor thinks it's unlikely. Provided you don't overdo things, he's sure you'll carry this baby full term.' She grinned at Denise. 'That means no stress, or worrying over what may never happen, right?'

Denise smiled shakily. 'You're right. I'm glad you could come for a visit, Jill. It's great to have another woman around the place.'

A twinge of guilt gripped Jill. If it hadn't been for her own need to get away from Perth, where she was a columnist for a national women's magazine, she wouldn't have come. Her brother and sister-in-law didn't know about her recent illness and the disaster it had caused.

Caught up with the hectic demands of their outback tourist property, Wildhaven, they had little time to read magazines, so they were unaware of what had happened. Denise thought Jill had simply decided to spend a few days with them in response to numerous invitations.

'I'm glad I came, too,' she said, aware of how much she meant it. Getting away from it all took on a whole new meaning in this rugged, barely inhabited corner of far north Western Australia. The nearest town was Wiluna, an arduous drive away over old mining roads where you could still see the corduroyed crossings of mulga logs which the early drovers had constructed in the mud to enable their cattle to cross.

Although called a desert, the area was far from being an endless sea of sand. It was dotted with ancient rocky outcrops, glassy white salt lakes, undulating gravel plains and shallow rock pools shaded by tall eucalyptus trees.

When Nick had told Jill he intended to buy the old pastoral lease and turn it into a sanctuary for injured wild animals, Jill had thought he was crazy. Now she wasn't so sure. Word of mouth was already putting Wildhaven on the tourist map. When the cabins were ready for overnight visitors, it might even be profitable. For now, occasional visitors were accommodated at the mud brick homestead, and considered themselves privileged. In deference to Denise's pregnancy, Jill was the only overnight guest at the moment.

'When does Tom get back?' she asked Denise. The young aboriginal stockman was Nick's right-hand man. An urgent family matter had taken him south, and Jill had taken over as many of his chores as she could manage. Feeding the calves was one of them.

Denise arched her back and gripped it with both hands, grimacing. 'Tomorrow, fortunately. I hate to see you doing so much, but——'

'Nonsense, I'm enjoying myself. It's just the change I needed.' No stress, no deadlines—and no accusing phone calls from a certain party who swore she had libelled him in her column, she thought ruefully.

'A change from what?' Denise prompted. 'I know something's the matter, Jill. I wish you'd confide in us. Maybe Nick and I could help.'

'Thanks for offering, but there's nothing, really,' Jill insisted. The last thing Denise needed was to share her worries, when she had enough of her own. She had already lost a child to a miscarriage, and was terrified of it happening again.

'Well, if you change your mind...' Denise let her voice trail away, then added briskly, 'How about some lunch? It seems as if we've fed everything around here except us.'

'Good idea, but I'll make it,' Jill said.

Denise shook her head. 'I volunteered Nick for the job of barbecue chef. The steaks are marinating and the salads are almost ready. All you have to do is round up the cook.'

Masculine voices told them there was no need to look far. Nick had been mending fences near the main entrance and was returning with another man in tow. Jill knew who he was the moment her eyes rested on his tall, broad figure, which all but blotted out the sun's glare.

As he approached, she took a quick inventory, matching the reality to his profile in her computer back at the office. In the flesh, he was much more prepossessing.

Flesh was the right word, she thought. His file listed him as six feet one inch tall, without revealing how much muscle and sinew could be packed into such a frame. It was positively daunting.

He wasn't handsome, she continued her inventory. Model looks would have been out of place on such a rugged individual. As he came closer, she decided that his nose was too long and his eyes were too black under ridiculously long lashes. His thick sable hair was cut a fraction too long with heavy locks sweeping across a high forehead. It added up to a disturbingly masculine package.

'Oh, no, not you,' she said in a furious undertone. How had he tracked her to Wildhaven?

Denise looked impressed. 'You know that hunk? And I don't mean my husband.'

Nick was a big, good-looking man, but his companion managed to make her brother look as if he should be thrown back in favour of bigger game.

'I know *of* him,' Jill said, gathering her wits with an effort. 'His name is Bryan McKinley.'

'The millionaire who owns half the north-west?' Denise sounded awed. 'I knew he lived out this way, but we don't move in such illustrious circles, I'm afraid.'

'Neither do I,' Jill conceded. 'I mean, we haven't actually met, but I—I wrote something about him in a recent column, and he wasn't too happy about it.'

Which was the understatement of the year. She had been compiling her annual Richter scale column of Australia's ten most eligible bachelors, based on reader polls. Bryan McKinley had topped every list.

But not her personal list, she thought angrily, remembering his arrogant response when she had called to secure an interview. Through a lackey he had said he didn't welcome such frivolous attention.

Frivolous! The thought still made her blood boil. Nevertheless, she had kept trying to contact him, only to receive a curt note threatening legal action if she didn't desist.

At least he had signed the note, she thought mutinously, only then recalling the tiny hand-written 'per' in front of the signature. Who did he think he was anyway?

What had followed would have been comical if it hadn't been so disastrous. Incensed by his arrogance, Jill had written a blistering five hundred words about the man, entirely from her own imagination. It wasn't meant to see the light of day and she had fully intended to wipe it from her computer after using it to let off steam.

What she hadn't anticipated was coming down with a particularly vicious virus which had laid her low the day the article was completed. Her doctor had prescribed some long overdue leave and her editor had concurred, offering to run a 'best of the Richter scale' series in her absence, after the bachelor story had appeared.

Therein lay the rub. While Jill had recuperated, a magazine staffer had edited Jill's copy on the eligible bachelors, inadvertently including the story on Bryan McKinley, which had duly appeared in print.

He didn't look like a man who was after her blood, she thought as he approached, chatting amiably to Nick. He could be paying a neighbourly call—neighbours being anyone within a thousand-mile radius out here.

But as soon as those dark eyes settled on her, she knew there was nothing neighbourly about the visit. A fire smouldered in his gaze, burning into her until she felt like a rabbit in a spotlight. There was no mistaking who was the hunter and whom the prey.

Every nerve-ending screamed a denial, even though logic insisted she was safe with her family. But was anywhere safe when Bryan McKinley was on the war-path?

It took every bit of courage she possessed to meet his gaze unwaveringly. For long, tension-studded minutes, he regarded her in silence, but when he spoke it was to voice an incongruous pleasantry.

'Good morning, ladies,' he said, touching a long-fingered hand to the wide brim of his Akubra hat. A darting glance silently excluded her from the appellation.

'This is Bryan McKinley from Bowana,' Nick introduced him. 'This is my wife, Denise, and my sister, Jill.'

Maybe the after-effects of the virus had heightened her imagination, Jill thought. Maybe Bryan didn't know who she was. His next words, husky with the dust of the outback, dispelled any such hope.

'Pleased to meet you both. I believe I already know Ms Richter by reputation.'

Denise glowed with sisterly pride. 'Jill has readers all over Australia.'

The dark gaze rested full on her, mocking laughter flashing in their depths. A muscle twitched in the granite jaw, as if he restrained himself with an effort. The man was laughing at her, Jill thought as murderous rage welled up inside her. He was enjoying every minute of this, playing her like a fish on a line. The problem was, what would happen when it was time to reel her in?

She decided to find out. 'I doubt whether Mr McKinley is a fan. There was a misunderstanding at the magazine, and something was printed by mistake which he isn't very happy about. I gather that's why you're here, Mr McKinley?'

'You flatter yourself. I came to talk to Nick and Denise about their work at Wildhaven.'

So much for her ego. Jill let out a heavy breath, until she realised he was still playing with her. If he thought he could attack her through her family, he was in for a surprise. 'Could I have a word with you in private?' she said, taking his arm so he had little choice but to move aside with her.

'Call me Bryan, please.' It was a little like trying to move a mountain, she thought, as he exerted just enough resistance to make it clear that he moved only because he wanted to.

When they were safely out of earshot she spat, 'What do you think you're playing at?'

'Visiting the neighbours. I'm interested in your brother's work.'

'I'll bet you are,' she threw at him in blatant disbelief. 'You're here because of my column, aren't you?'

The look he turned on her was stripped of all pretence of civility. 'Are you surprised?'

Masking her nervousness, she retorted, 'I'm surprised you didn't send a lackey like the last couple of times. How did you find me anyway?'

'Your magazine was remarkably helpful once I identified myself. Your column has made your editor somewhat nervous. She was most anxious to assist me.'

Jill's editor had been away when the column appeared, but had telephoned Jill as soon as she returned. Confessing the mistake, Jill had voiced the opinion that the article, while unflattering, was so obviously tongue-in-cheek that no harm should come of it. Now Bryan's call had jeopardised everything. 'Did you tell her you mean to sue?' she asked shakily.

'I reserved the possibility.'

'But you can't. My column is written as personal opinion and, as such, I'm surely entitled to it?'

His eyebrows tilted ominously. 'There are limits to what is acceptable as opinion, as you're well aware. It doesn't seem to have occurred to you that I have better things to do than participate in your farcical poll.'

A red mist floated across her eyes. 'You may call it farcical, but my readers take it very seriously.'

'Furthermore,' he continued as if she hadn't interjected, 'I felt it was inappropriate to send an assistant to collect the apology which you owe me.'

Her hair spun in a glossy curtain as she shook her head wildly. His arrogance took her breath away. In other circumstances, she might have apologised, but his blatant assumption that the fault was all on her side drove her on to the defensive. 'You treated me appallingly. Why should I be the one to apologise?'

'There are ways I could convince you.'

She shot an anxious glance at Denise, who was leaning against a sliprail, chatting to Nick. A chill settled over Jill. 'Isn't suing the magazine enough?'

'I didn't say I was going to sue—yet. I have several possible alternatives.'

The colour drained from her face as he followed the direction of her glance to Nick and Denise. Her hands twisted together in unconscious supplication. 'Look, I don't know what you have in mind, but you'd better leave my family out of it. For the baby's sake, Denise has to avoid stress at all costs.'

'Then you'll have to make sure she does, won't you?'

'What do you mean?'

'I'm sure an intelligent woman like you can figure it out.'

The hairs rose on the back of her neck. 'You can't expect me to act as if your visit is welcome.'

He nodded, strands of sable hair falling across his eyes. He brushed them aside, the gesture oddly appealing, as if there was at least one thing about him which wasn't under iron control. 'I can and I do. I gather you haven't told them what happened?'

'I didn't want Denise worrying about me.' Or about you, she thought. She wished he would state what he wanted from her and go.

Her own reactions were part of the problem, she realised. It was probably a result of the virus, but he made her feel extraordinarily vulnerable.

Butterflies danced in her stomach and it was an effort to keep her mind on what he was saying.

'Nick asked me to stay for lunch,' he informed her levelly.

Horror winged its way across her face. 'You haven't accepted?'

'They'd think it strange if I didn't. I'd advise you to compose yourself and start acting as if you're delighted to see me, before they suspect that something is wrong between us.'

'I can't do it alone,' she retorted, knowing exactly how a cornered animal felt.

'I hardly expect you to. Don't you trust me to behave like a gentleman, in deference to your sister-in-law's condition? Or are you afraid I'll behave like a "tinpot tycoon with delusions of sainthood"?'

She flinched as he threw the quote from the column at her, but managed not to show it, shrugging with apparent nonchalance instead. 'If the cap fits——'

'An assessment you are hardly qualified to make,' he cut in coldly.

Her temper flared, although all the signs warned her to beware. 'And whose fault is that? I tried for an interview, but you didn't even have the guts to turn me down personally.'

The shadowed line along his jaw tightened and a frown etched a valley across his deep forehead. 'So now I'm gutless as well. This promises to be a fascinating afternoon.'

It promised to be more like slow torture. For her sister-in-law's sake she would have to survive it somehow. If only she hadn't chosen Wildhaven as her bolt-hole. It was too close to the devil's lair. She had known that Bryan McKinley owned huge tracts of land in the north-west, but had foolishly assumed that the area was large enough for both of them. Now she knew better.

She tensed as Nick joined them. 'If you two have finished your private discussion, I'll show you around the place, Bryan.'

He nodded. 'Ready when you are.'

'By the time we've done the rounds, the girls will have lunch on the table.'

Bryan's look seared Jill. 'I don't want to put the *girls* to any trouble.'

Jill's look was designed to melt steel. 'It's no trouble at all. You *boys* enjoy yourselves.'

Her anger slid off him. 'I'm already enjoying this far more than I thought I would.'

The nerve of the man! Jill was shaking with anger by the time Nick and Bryan McKinley walked away. So he was enjoying this, was he? She felt as if she were being turned slowly on a spit over hot coals. And all because of one stupid slip in print for which he was as much to blame as she was.

'You look as if you'd like to murder someone,' Denise commented, studying Jill's face in concern.

For her sister-in-law's sake, Jill schooled her features into an impassive mask. 'Don't you mind being called a girl? I'm twenty-nine years old, for goodness' sake!' Bryan was only a couple of years older, she recalled from her research.

Denise flipped her sunhat off and massaged her chin where the elastic had chafed. 'You get used to it out here. We women are always "the girls" to our menfolk. This is Big Man Country, remember?'

Jill smiled fondly at her sister-in-law. 'No wonder my brother loves outback life. He can be king in his castle. It's positively feudal. You can't tell me a woman couldn't run a cattle station.'

'They can and do,' Denise said mildly, linking arms to draw Jill towards the homestead. 'Who do you think held everything together while the men were driving cattle along the stock routes to the railheads in the old days?'

'All the same, I don't see why we have to pander to their fragile egos while we're doing it.'

'Did you have any particular ego in mind?' Denise asked innocently.

Jill gave her an equally bland look. 'Why do you ask?' She couldn't resist a backward glance to where Nick was showing Bryan a dingo pup which was recovering from a road accident which had killed its mother. What was Bryan telling Nick? She would never forgive him if he dragged her family into their private quarrel.

She was still worrying as they prepared salad vegetables for lunch. Having given up on her barbecue cook, Denise had thrown the steaks on to a vast indoor hotplate where they sizzled and sparked, sending out mouth-watering aromas.

Where was Nick? How long did it take to do the rounds of a few animals pens? If Bryan said anything to upset either Nick or Denise, Jill would . . . Tomato seeds spattered the room as her cleaver slammed down on the chopping board.

Beside her, Denise jumped. 'Jill!'

Shaken by the vehemence of her thoughts, Jill put the cleaver down and began to mop up the mess. 'Sorry, my mind was elsewhere.'

'Are you sure you aren't in love?'

Oh, heavens, Denise was already reading too much into Bryan's unexpected arrival. 'It isn't what you're thinking,' she cautioned. 'Bryan came to see me about a business matter, so don't get your hopes up.'

'Pity. He'd make a wonderful brother-in-law, and I'd love a playmate for Nick junior.' She patted her rounded stomach lovingly.

If Denise knew the real situation between her and Bryan, she would be horrified, Jill thought. The very idea of being involved with him, sharing his bed and bearing his children was...was...she didn't even want to think about it.

But it was the curse of an active imagination that it conjured up images almost against her will. This time they were so vivid that a wave of heat swept through her. She was actually picturing herself in bed with Bryan, when it was the last place she should want to be.

'How can you be sure it isn't Nicola junior?' she asked in a determined effort to change the subject.

'Because it's over-active, unreasonably demanding and delights in making my life difficult,' Denise replied.

Which described Bryan to a T. 'You're right; it's definitely male,' Jill concurred.

'What have we done this time?' Nick demanded, joining them in the kitchen.

Without turning around, Jill was aware of Bryan close behind him. Even before he spoke, something about him triggered a sensory red alert throughout her system.

'You know the old saying,' he drawled, ' "They can't do with us, and they can't do without us".'

Want to bet? Jill thought mutinously. There was one man she definitely could do without, but he showed no signs of leaving. She had a feeling his words were as much for her as for Nick.

'I wouldn't be too sure,' she said with exaggerated sweetness. Her sharp turn made the dressing from the coleslaw she carried flick across Bryan's knitted shirt which stretched across his broad chest, delineating muscles she hadn't known a man possessed.

He looked down at the white tracery marring his shirt, and danger signals flashed in the dark eyes. Later, his look seemed to say. Immediately she regretted her reckless impulse. Playing with fire felt like an apt description.

But he only reached a finger to one of the droplets, gathered some dressing, and transferred it to his mouth, being deliberately provocative, she was sure. 'Tasty,' he murmured. 'Dessert should be most interesting.'

'There isn't any,' she hissed under her breath, furious with herself for letting him have such a disturbing effect on her.

'Then I'll have to take what's going, won't I?'

Her traitorous imagination supplied another vivid image of herself on a silver platter, an apple clenched in her jaws. She knew exactly what—or, rather, whom—he had in mind for dessert. 'Forget it. There's lemon meringue pie,' she amended hastily.

'Pity.'

Yes, wasn't it? In a fury, she followed the others on to the screened veranda which overlooked a spring-fed bore where water-birds waded in the shallows. The plates of steaks and salads were ferried out, and Jill was the last to take her seat, horrified to find that Denise had seated her beside Bryan. If she hadn't been pregnant...

'How did you two happen to meet?' the object of Jill's furious thoughts asked sweetly.

Jill's heart began to hammer against her ribs as she waited for Bryan's answer. He could hardly tell the truth. If he said anything to upset Denise, she would kill him.

'Actually, we hadn't met before today,' he supplied, well aware of how she tensed beside him. 'Our first meetings were by phone for Jill's annual bachelor poll.'

'And are you a ten on the Richter scale?' Denise asked, oblivious of the warning looks Jill flashed at her. I know what I'm doing and you'll thank me later, her mild expression seemed to say.

Jill gave up and munched on a piece of steak which had turned to cardboard in her mouth.

'According to Jill, I'm off the scale,' he said drily. 'Tell them what else you said about me, Jill.'

Choking on her steak, she felt his palm crash against the small of her back, and the offending piece of meat dislodged itself. 'There's no need to beat me to a pulp,' she snapped at him. His hand lingered against her spine, sending waves of heat along it.

'Sorry, I forget my own strength sometimes,' he said, without a hint of real apology. She had a feeling that Bryan McKinley never forgot his own

strength. Or his opponent's weaknesses. He handed
her a glass of water which she took with little grace.

'You were going to tell us what you said about
Bryan in your column,' Denise went on relentlessly.

She gave him her sweetest look. 'Modesty forbids
me repeating it. I wouldn't want to embarrass our
guest.'

Her answer finally satisfied Denise and the conversation moved on to other topics. Unwillingly,
Jill's gaze was drawn again and again to Bryan as
he discussed Nick's plans for the wildlife refuge.

Only the cynical gleam in his eyes when he looked
her way served as a reminder of his avowed intention to take revenge on Jill for the column. But
how? When? Waiting for the answers tied her
stomach in knots. Fortunately, only Bryan seemed
aware of her growing tension as the meal
progressed.

'I'll fetch the dessert,' she said when Denise
began to rise. She welcomed any excuse to escape
from Bryan's presence.

He thwarted her by reaching across the table to
gather up the plates. 'I'll give you a hand.'

'I can manage, thank you,' she said through
clenched teeth, but was hardly surprised when he
followed her into the kitchen and began loading the
plates into the dishwasher. Taking no for an answer
obviously wasn't his strong suit.

As she got out the dessert plates and began to
slice the huge lemon meringue pie, she was aware
of him watching her every move.

'Your brother and sister-in-law are an impressive
couple,' he said, surprising her.

'I agree,' she said warily, wondering where he was leading.

'I gather that the park is Nick's life.'

'You gather correctly. He gave up a career as a veterinarian and sold everything he owned to buy Wildhaven. It's his dream.'

Bryan folded his arms across his broad chest, his expression impassive. 'It's rare to find people with a dream these days, especially one they're willing to give up everything to realise.'

She straightened, wiping creamy hands on a towel. 'So you see why I don't want to burden them with our disagreement? They have more than enough on their plate with the baby coming, and trying to make the park pay its way. As it is, the land is mortgaged to the hilt.'

'I know. One of my nominee companies holds the mortgage. We finance a lot of developments in the north-west, so it was one of the first things I checked when I found out where you'd gone to ground.'

When he went looking for a weapon to use against her, she supplied the rest. 'Does Nick know?' she asked tautly.

'Obviously he knows who holds his mortgage, but not that the company is under my control. I see no need to enlighten him for the moment.'

'For the moment? You wouldn't use your influence to get back at me through him, would you? It wouldn't be fair to them.'

'Your column was hardly fair to me.'

'But to threaten an innocent couple's livelihood over something which wasn't their fault... How could you?'

He spread his hands wide. 'Anything is possible for a tinpot tycoon with delusions of sainthood.'

She clutched her hands to her temples. 'I'm sorry I ever wrote such a thing. I was so wrong.'

'Then you admit it?'

Raising glittering eyes to him, she nodded. 'Oh, yes. I was wrong. I didn't go nearly far enough in my condemnation of you. You don't have delusions of sainthood at all. How could you, when you're in league with the devil himself?'

He shook his head. 'You still don't get it, do you? Your words are useless against me. They can't hurt me.'

He wasn't making sense. 'Then why are you here?'

Before he could answer, Nick backed into the kitchen, his arms laden with salad bowls. 'Thought I'd see what's keeping dessert.'

As Nick turned around, Bryan swept Jill into his arms, stifling her instinctive protest with the force of his lips possessing hers.

'Oops, sorry. I'll come back later.'

The door had closed behind Nick for several seconds before Bryan saw fit to release her. And not before he had plundered her mouth in a way which left her breathless and shaken. She had been kissed before, but never with such unbridled passion. His touch was like fire, and every nerve-ending in her body flared instantly in response, before she regained control of herself.

Turning herself to stone in his arms, she turned her head aside. 'You bastard. You had no right to do that. If this is your idea of revenge . . .'

Taking his time, he freed her, the mocking amusement back in his expression. 'My idea of revenge goes much, much further. This is a mere foretaste of what you can expect. In the interests of keeping the truth from your family, naturally.'

'Naturally.' If looks could kill, he would be dead where he stood. 'You didn't have to go this far,' she seethed, confused by the intensity of her reaction. Was she angry with Bryan for kissing her, or with herself for the uninhibited way she had responded?

To her chagrin, he was well aware of it. How could he not be, when sparks had arced back and forth between them in the split second of body contact? A lightning strike lasted for mere seconds, but it left an indelible mark. If she checked the soles of her feet, would they be smouldering?

He chuckled softly, the sound driving her into a greater fury. 'I haven't gone nearly as far as I intend to with you, Jill. You're taking on the wrong man.'

Suddenly weary of the chase, she slumped against the kitchen table. 'All right, you win. Sue me for everything I've got. I've had enough of your cat-and-mouse game. And especially of being the mouse.'

He looked genuinely surprised. 'Suing you is much too easy. All I'd get out of you in a court of law would be money.'

'If it isn't money you want, then what is it?'

'Haven't you guessed yet? The only thing I want is you.'

CHAPTER TWO

THE knife she was using to slice the pie trembled in her hand, visions of plunging it into his heart filling her mind. It wouldn't be hygienic. The blade was sticky with lemon meringue.

Slowly she lowered the knife, her journalist's mind picturing the headline. Cause of demise? Lemon meringue poisoning. It was too mundane an ending for a man like Bryan McKinley. A cattle stampede was more his style, the gorier the better. She drew herself up to her full height, still unable to meet more than his infuriatingly sardonic mouth. 'You can't be serious. My crime wasn't as heinous as all that.'

His jaw tightened. 'You think not? Your thoughtless article caused more harm than you can possibly know, including interfering in some investment plans of mine.'

'Investment plans?' When in doubt, echo the previous statement, she recalled her communications theory. His assertion that she had done some real harm had shaken her far more than she was willing to let him see.

'Exactly. I'm involved with a foreign consortium to bring a major tourist development to the northwest. It will provide badly needed jobs and investment. Negotiations were at a delicate stage when your article appeared.'

Nervously she licked meringue off her fingers. If he wanted to make her feel guilty, he was succeeding magnificently. 'I don't see how one article could make that much difference,' she said defensively.

'Ordinarily it wouldn't, but my associates are somewhat publicity-shy. Your childish poll couldn't have come at a worse time for them.'

He was doing it again, disparaging her work. 'It wasn't childish,' she seethed. 'It's a perfectly valid means of expressing an opinion.'

'One you would have done better to keep to yourself,' he snapped. 'Thankfully, I shall be able to restore their confidence in the integrity of our media with time and patience, but until then the project is on hold, mostly thanks to you.'

Her strangled breath sounded loud in the quiet kitchen. 'But how did they find out?' Her magazine wasn't circulated outside the country and was hardly likely to interest the foreign business community.

His broad shoulders sloped eloquently. 'It hardly matters to the end result, but the article was sent to them with a covering letter designed to undermine the project even further.'

So it wasn't only her column which did the damage. 'Then you can hardly hold me responsible for the entire fiasco,' she denied hotly. 'I wasn't the one who sent it to your associates.'

'But you were the one who wrote it,' he said with dangerous intensity. 'Now the time has come to pay the piper.'

Having already endured a taste of his idea of payment, Jill suppressed a tremor. Her nerves tightened as he stretched the silence to the fullest, maximising her discomfort, she was sure. Her tongue darted out to lick arid lips as she bit back the retort which sprang to mind. There was no point in giving him even more ammunition against her.

It was obvious that he knew quite well what form he wanted his 'payment' to take and he was waiting for her to beg to know the nature of her punishment. Well, she was damned if she would utter a word.

'Not even curious?' he drawled, his eyes glinting a challenge.

'Since I don't have to do anything you say, why should I be?' she asked, keeping her voice steady with an effort.

His bladed hand slashed the air. 'Then you'd rather take the consequences?'

Tears glittered on her lashes, but she refused to shed them. Nevertheless, she knew he had won. She couldn't let him harm Nick and Denise. 'No,' she admitted in a tone of surrender. 'Damn you, what do you have in mind?'

'That you work your penance in Bowana. The tourist development is designed to provide jobs for the young people, enabling them to stay in the area, and boosting the farmers' incomes in hard times. Since the project is held up because of you, you're going to find another way to bring tourists to the town in the meantime.'

He couldn't be serious, although she was horribly afraid that he was. 'I don't know the first thing about tourism,' she denied.

'But you do know the media. The right kind of publicity is the key to success in a venture like this.'

'I'm not a publicist. I'm a magazine columnist.'

His gaze hardened. 'Before that you worked for
an advertising agency as a copywriter, later account executive. Your clients included shopping
centres, a radio station and a cruise company.'

Acid rose in her throat. 'You've been checking
up on me. How could you invade my privacy so
callously?'

He dismissed her anger with a gesture. 'The same
way you invaded mine with your column.'

'That was different. That was research.'

'Calling it research makes it respectable, I
suppose. Damn it, you think it's OK to dig around
in other people's private lives, but it hurts when
someone digs around in yours, doesn't it?'

Colour flooded her cheeks. 'Yes.'

'Then be thankful I'm not inclined to publicise
your activities. Your latest affair would make fascinating reading.'

'It wasn't an affair,' she shot back. How had he
found out about David Hockey? 'David is a col-
league and we went out a few times. When I found
out that he was still married, and not separated as
I'd believed, I stopped seeing him.'

'Commendable of you,' Bryan sneered. 'It took
you what, three months, to find out that he still
had a wife?'

'She was overseas for most of those three
months.' She brushed a lock of hair away from her
eyes, the gesture mirroring her frustration. 'I'm sure
I'm not the first woman to be duped by a married
man.'

'Probably not even the first to be duped by that
particular married man,' he commented cynically.

'If you know so much, then you must know I'm the wrong person to help you save your town,' she threw at him.

'On the contrary, you're the ideal person to do it. I'd say a month's commitment would be enough to redress the damage you've caused.'

Her jaw dropped. How could she possibly work with him for a month? 'I can't. I have my job with the magazine.'

'They can do without you for four weeks. Your editor assures me you have that much leave accrued.'

'You've thought of everything, haven't you?' she demanded bitterly.

His expression was impassive. 'I usually do.' He picked up the pie she'd been mechanically serving. 'We'll settle the details after lunch.'

'There's no point; I'm not coming,' she insisted, but with the uncomfortable feeling that he had already won. The swing-door between the kitchen and the dining-room rocked gently, mocking her denial which he hadn't even heard.

'I'm not coming,' she whispered to the closed door. He couldn't force her to, could he? Yes, he could, she acknowledged, slumping against a cupboard. As long as he controlled the mortgage over her brother's property, he controlled her. And he knew it, damn him.

She had no doubt that he would use any weapon at his disposal if she didn't co-operate. And she couldn't let him hurt Nick and Denise because of her. She had never hated anyone as much as she hated Bryan McKinley at that moment.

Thinking of the insolent way his eyes had devoured her, she shuddered. There must be some way to satisfy his conditions without going to his town herself. She didn't like the way her body responded to his presence almost independently of her will. Going with him would be like walking into the lion's den. There must be another way.

The others had almost finished dessert when she rejoined them, bringing the coffee-pot to excuse her delay. 'Now I know how you keep trim,' Denise observed. 'Keep busy during dessert.'

Jill avoided Bryan's eyes, although she could feel the heat of his gaze on her. Well, let him look. She was proud of her trim figure, honed through regular sessions of aerobics and as much walking as she could fit into her busy life. With an appetite like hers, Jill needed all the help she could get.

'You should try this pie. It's delicious.' Bryan pushed the last slice of lemon meringue towards her.

If Nick or Denise had offered, she would have weakened, but refusing Bryan was easy. With a look which told him she wouldn't accept food from him during a famine, she pushed the plate back. 'I can't accept, really.' They both knew she didn't mean the pie.

His dark eyes mocked her. 'You might find it more to your liking than you think.'

'I'd probably choke on it.'

'Dear me, I hope you don't mean my cooking.' Denise sounded alarmed.

'Of course not. Bryan meant something else.'

Nick grinned broadly, no doubt thinking of the scene he'd interrupted in the kitchen. Jill's swift kick under the table banished the grin before he could make a facetious comment. Instead, he took a swallow of coffee.

Since she could hardly kick Denise, it was her sister-in-law who asked, 'What do you have in mind, Bryan?'

'Jill's thinking of coming to Bowana to help develop the place for tourism,' he said blandly. 'I'll be leaving first thing tomorrow. We can drive north in convoy.'

Panic flashed through her before she mastered it. It seemed she had little choice but to co-operate. At least she wouldn't have to share a car with Bryan through the long drive, and she could leave when ready. She was ready now, she acknowledged to herself. But as long as he held the mortgage to Wildhaven, she was trapped. 'You have everything worked out, haven't you?' she asked in an acid tone.

'It pays in the outback,' he assured her. He pushed his chair back from the table. 'If you'll excuse me, I have calls to make. I'll see you in the morning, Jill.' He named a time which made her gasp.

'That's practically the crack of dawn.'

'It's the best time to travel these roads.' He planted his Akubra hat far back on his head and touched two fingers to it, saying to Denise, 'Thanks for the lunch.'

Denise smiled warmly. 'Any friend of Jill's is welcome any time, Bryan. You'll see your guest out, won't you, Jill?'

Seething inwardly, Jill stalked to the door and let it slam behind her, cutting Bryan off. Tut-tutting softly, he pushed it open and moved up behind her, resting his hands on her shoulders. 'Is that any way to treat a friend?'

She wished his hands didn't feel like brands, fiery through her T-shirt. 'I didn't want to upset Denise, but I'd hardly call us friends. I can't possibly come to Bowana tomorrow, but I can talk to some people in Perth about the tourism idea. They may be able to help.'

None too gently he turned her to face him and his eyes burned into her. They were like hot coals, and she flinched from the heat which threatened to sear her soul. 'You owe me this, Jill, and you're going to pay. You personally, not your friends back in the city.'

What had happened to her heart? Suddenly it was beating double time, hammering an alarming tattoo against her ribs. Her breath tangled in her throat. 'You can't make me come with you.'

He glanced back towards the house. 'Are you quite sure about that?'

'But if I don't, you'll make things hard for Nick and Denise. What kind of a man are you, threatening innocent people in order to get your own way?'

His forefinger traced a lazy line along her jaw and down the side of her throat, connecting with the throbbing pulse-point in her neck. He let the hand linger there a moment, as if taking the measure of her inner turmoil. 'When you get to Bowana, you'll find out what kind of man I am.'

His mouth hovered tantalisingly close, the cleft between nose and lips deeply shadowed. There was another shadow in the cleft of his chin, inviting her touch to see if the valleys were as deep as they seemed. She shook his hand away. 'You don't leave me much choice, do you?'

His smile ravished her. 'I don't think you really want me to.'

She found her voice with an effort. 'Of all the arrogant, presumptuous . . .' But it was too late. He was already halfway to his car. She heard him humming under his breath.

So he thought she wanted to go with him, did he? Her column had been right all along. He was a tinpot tycoon with delusions of...of... Sainthood hardly fitted any more. He was no candidate for canonisation. Boiling in oil would be too good for him.

She refused to fuel his ego by watching him drive away, but as she spun around she bumped into Nick, emerging from the house. 'Are all outback men as tyrannical as Bryan McKinley?' she demanded furiously.

Nick laughed. 'Probably not. His success didn't come by being soft-hearted.'

'To be soft-hearted, you need to have a heart in the first place,' she flung back, trying to ignore the sound of an engine revving. Nick waved, and it was all she could do not to turn around and watch Bryan leave. Good riddance to him, she tried to tell herself. Maybe he'd drive his car into a tree and be in plaster from neck to knee for the next three months, so she wouldn't have to go with him tomorrow.

'See you at dawn, Jill,' she heard him say, and knew that no tree would dare stand in Bryan McKinley's way.

'Not if I see you first,' she muttered under her breath.

Her brother chuckled. 'Well, well. It seems my dear sister has finally met her match.'

She gave him a horrified look. 'Me and that . . . that back-woodsman? You must be joking.'

'I wouldn't underestimate Bryan,' he cautioned her. 'He can muster stocks and shares as efficiently as he musters cattle, so don't be fooled by the casual shirt and jeans. He runs his cattle stations as businesses, from his headquarters in Bowana.'

'Next thing you'll be telling me he takes in widows and orphans.'

Nick rested his hands against the veranda railing. 'For all I know, he might. You have to admit, he's an improvement on some of the wimps you've been seeing.'

Colour flamed in her cheeks. She and Nick had been best friends all their lives, clinging to one another rather than risk making other friends when their father, an outback policeman, moved from one posting to another. She had never suspected that he disapproved of her men friends. 'David Hockey wasn't a wimp,' she denied.

'But he was married. Face it, little sister, you're one high-powered lady. You need a man who's at least your equal.'

Like Bryan McKinley? she wondered. 'I'm not sure I care to be labelled ''high-powered'',' she said.

He frowned. 'It isn't meant as a criticism. But you earn more than most men do. You have your own town house in Perth and you've travelled all over. How many men can match, far less exceed, your achievements?'

She touched the back of her hand to his cheek. 'You can, big brother. And I don't mean in net worth. What you're doing here is worth far more than anything I've done up to now.'

'Then maybe Bryan's right. A challenge like saving Bowana is what you need.'

'Never.' She swore under her breath. How could Nick imagine that she wanted to be involved with a heartless tyrant like Bryan McKinley, no matter how noble his cause? She would rather die!

She wondered if Nick would think Bryan so wonderful if he knew that the other man held the mortgage to Wildhaven as surety for her co-operation.

All the same, he *was* a ten on the Richter scale, she thought contrarily. If only she hadn't included him in her frivolous annual survey, she wouldn't be in this predicament now. Oh, the joys of hindsight, she reminded herself. His photo had screamed 'ten' at her from the beginning.

In fact, it was hard to remember anything at all about the other nine men, she realised. There was the son of a mining magnate and—er—the presenter of a current affairs programme. Darn it, why couldn't she bring them to mind when she'd dated at least three of them at different times?

The symptoms of the virus must be bothering her still, she decided. It was the only acceptable reason why one bachelor should dominate her mind to the exclusion of all the rest.

CHAPTER THREE

'AND no more kissing, understand?'

The moment Bryan's gaze dipped to her full lips, made glossy with sunscreen cream, she regretted raising the subject of kissing. It was an instant, painful reminder of a moment she'd prefer to forget. Instead, her errant mind went into an action-replay of his hand pressed against her spine while he took advantage of her surprise to commandeer her mouth.

His face reflected cynical amusement. 'There's no need, since we won't have your brother and sister-in-law to impress. Besides, driving in the desert doesn't leave much time for other diversions.'

'I'm hardly a diversion,' she seethed, furious to hear the kiss dismissed so lightly when it had haunted her throughout a restless night. Searching for a reason, she had finally blamed his high-handedness. No one had ever treated her so arrogantly. Instead of helping to shield Denise from the real reason for his visit, he had been helping himself—to her.

His chin was shadowed, as if he hadn't shaved before coming to collect her, and he massaged the rough skin. 'As a man, I disagree. You're enough to divert the concentration of any red-blooded male.'

Despite the dawn coolness, she felt her face grow warm. 'Am I supposed to be flattered? Next you'll be saying it was all my fault. Some men just don't know how to take no for an answer.'

His dark eyes gleamed. 'I can take no for an answer, provided it isn't a disguised yes.'

'I don't recall being given a choice either way.'

How had the conversation shifted on to such personal ground so quickly? All she'd tried to do was to establish some ground rules before they set off. It seemed reasonable. She knew him only by reputation, and if she believed even half of it she would be crazy to go with him. Obviously she didn't believe it all. Yet he had already taken advantage of an awkward situation. What was to stop him doing it again, when they were miles from civilisation?

He pushed his wide-brimmed hat back and fanned long fingers through the dark hair trailing across his forehead. 'You had a choice, and you made it.'

He was implying that she had not only accepted but enjoyed his kiss. 'Of all the conceited . . .'

His angry look chilled her into silence. 'More compliments, Jill? Aren't you afraid of provoking a big-headed bully?'

Her intended insult died on her lips as he quoted another line from her column with dangerous emphasis, affirming her own worst fears. Oh, why couldn't she have deleted the article before she became ill?

For a moment she thought longingly of turning around and driving back to Perth, until she remembered what was at stake. How could she leave her family's fate in the hands of such a ruthless man?

His hand clamped around her wrist, turning her to face him. 'Don't even think of running away. We have an agreement and I intend to hold you to it.'

The ferocity of his grip made her eyes glisten. How had he known what she was thinking? 'I'm not a coward,' she said softly. 'I'll come to your town and do my best for you, but that's *all* I'll do.'

'It's all I'm asking you to do.'

He released her and she made a show of rubbing her wrist, although there was no real pain. He had gauged his strength precisely. She debated whether to try for the last word, then thought better of it. The verbal sparring was only making her uncomfortably aware of him as a man.

Not that she needed reminding. She had only to let her eyes dwell on the breadth of his shoulders and travel down his arms to where his rolled-back shirt-sleeves hugged work-hardened biceps. His moleskin trousers rode low on narrow hips, the taut material creased with desert dust into folds which practically advertised his masculinity.

Annoyed with herself, she tore her gaze away. 'Then let's get this over with.'

He had already checked her four-wheel-drive car, reducing the pressure in the tyres to cope with the sand dunes which lay ahead of them. She had protested when he insisted on removing the protection plates under the vehicle body. 'Won't I need them if we have to cross rocky terrain or creeks?' she protested.

He had climbed underneath and removed the plates anyway, then showed them to her. 'This sharp edge will mow down all the spinifex which grows

between the wheel tracks. Inside an hour you'll have
so much spinifex in there, you'll have to take the
plates off anyway. By then the car will have generated enough heat to set the whole mess on fire.'

'Oh.'

'Yes, oh.' Her ignorance of such matters was
monumental, but surprisingly he didn't rub it in.
Instead, he continued his methodical checking until
he was satisfied with their small convoy. 'Right,
we're off, then.'

She said goodbye to Nick and Denise, who
promised to keep in touch by radio telephone. 'Have
fun,' Denise called as Jill swung herself into the
driver's seat and followed in Bryan's dusty wake.

She managed a smile and a wave, but her heart
sank. Some fun it was going to be, ploughing over
mountainous sand dunes and through car-eating
grasses to get to a one-horse town she was supposed to save single-handedly. 'Take it easy,' her
doctor had prescribed. She doubted that this was
what she'd had in mind.

She had to admit the desert was a beautiful sight.
As they left Wildhaven behind, the first rays of sun
turned the sand blood-red and stained the clumps
of spinifex with lilac and gold.

The going was rough, and her arms began to ache
from fighting the steering-wheel. Her teeth chat-
tered as she jolted over a cattle grid. As she changed
into four-wheel-drive for the umpteenth time, she
began to wonder when they would stop for a break.
She dared not risk letting his car out of sight, but
her throat was parched from the dust forcing its
way into the cabin through every crevice, and gritty

from the spinifex seeds the cooling system dragged into the car.

Bryan had been right about the spinifex. Every few miles they had to stop and pull handfuls of it out of every nook and cranny. Heavy gloves were needed to clean the car's red-hot exhaust system. A fire wasn't hard to imagine.

The road was little more than wheel indentations in the sand. More of a guide was the fence line they followed north-east along the southern bank of a dry creek. They seemed to be heading for a pass in the rock hills. In the shimmering heat, it was impossible to guess how far away it was.

Her patience was at a low ebb by the time he swung his car off the road on to the barest hint of a side-track. A few kilometres later she pulled up beside him and climbed stiffly out of the car. 'Good grief, is it a mirage?'

The pool was vast and ringed by stands of majestic river-red gums. An ochre-coloured outcrop of rock bordered the far side. Clouds of finches and budgerigars swooped and dived to drink.

'Looks like one, but it isn't. It's a favourite local swimming-pool and watering-hole for the stock from the nearby station.'

'If this is private property, won't the owners object to us stopping here?'

His mouth twitched. 'The owner won't object. He and I are intimately acquainted.'

'*You* own this land?'

'It's one of three properties owned by McKinley Pastoral Company,' he said, obviously enjoying her reaction.

Since he owned the company, the answer was the same, but she refused to let him see how impressed she was. 'So why not hire a public relations firm to do your dirty work? You could probably afford to buy one, if the truth be known.'

'I'm sorry you think that providing a future for a town's youth is dirty work.'

Instantly she regretted her outburst. 'Of course I don't. But I'm not thrilled about being dragged out here against my will.'

He rested his back against the jeep and folded his arms. 'You mean you'd have come if I asked you politely?'

She removed her hat and lifted the heavy mass of hair off her hot neck with a sigh. 'Since I can't imagine you doing any such thing, you'll have to wonder, won't you?'

Without answering, he strode to the water's edge and dipped his bandanna into it, wringing it out as he stood up. Before she knew what was happening, he had pressed the cool compress against her neck. 'Better?'

A delicious shudder rippled through her. Was it at the coolness, or the touch of his work-roughened palm against her nape? Before she could decide, he returned to the pool and splashed water on to his face.

When he straightened, the water made rivulets in the dust caking his features. Unshaven, he looked like a bushranger, the highway robbers who used to hold up travellers and demand their gold.

Some bushrangers carried off women, she re-called. Wild love in a wild land. She shook herself mentally. The heat must be distorting her thinking.

'Don't you believe in shaving?' she demanded, taking her irritation out on the nearest thing handy, which happened to be him.

Her ire left him unmoved. 'I do if I consider the occasion important enough.'

So today was unimportant in his scheme of things. The idea rankled and she turned aside, rummaging in the back of her car for the well-padded box of supplies Denise had insisted she take along. 'Denise packed us some coffee. How do you like yours?'

'What happened to your much vaunted research?' he challenged her. 'You should know the answer—hot and strong.'

'If you say "like my women" I may just throw this at you,' she warned as his barbed response hit home.

'Then I won't say it,' he complied. He didn't need to. The confirmation was in his taunting look as she handed him a plastic mug filled with the fragrant brew. He would prefer women who were at home in this harsh brown land, she thought. It would probably help to be in awe of Bryan McKinley, too. She didn't qualify on either count.

'When do we get to Bowana?' she asked between sips of coffee.

'In a hurry? I thought tomorrow would be soon enough.'

'Tomorrow?' She choked on the drink, moving hastily out of reach before he could administer another bone-jarring thump on her back. 'I'm not camping out in this wilderness with you.'

He made a sweeping gesture. 'You don't have a choice.'

'But I can't. It isn't...'

Safe was what she meant, although it was debatable which of them she was afraid to trust. 'Decent?' he supplied with a mocking look. 'You're a liberated woman. Why should you care what anyone else thinks?'

'Being liberated can also mean being fussy about the company one keeps,' she threw at him.

'Too true, but I'll try to grin and bear it.'

'I should think that spending a night with me would do wonders for your reputation,' she said, furious at having her words twisted. Then her face flamed as she realised what she'd said. 'Not that you'll get any such chance,' she added belatedly.

He finished his coffee and shook out the dregs on to the dry ground. 'Pity. It's the best invitation I've had in a long time.'

'In your dreams.' At the same time, a contrary part of her imagination insisted on picturing two sleeping-bags drawn up beside a flickering campfire. The bags would be close together for warmth or maybe even zipped into one. Desert nights could be chilly.

Stop it, she commanded her thoughts. That vision was as much a mirage as the lake had seemed to be.

'Then we'd better try to make Bowana by nightfall, hadn't we?'

Contrarily, disappointment stabbed her as she realised they wouldn't be camping out after all. Then her annoyance grew. He'd been testing her, and she'd fallen for it all the way. She schooled her features into a tolerant mask. 'I guessed as much. I looked up the distance on the map last night. But

I let you have your little joke. Boys will be boys,
won't they?'

Something flickered in his dark gaze. It tele-
graphed a warning which Jill heeded too late. Her
hesitant step backwards was arrested by the clamp
of his hands on her upper arms. His fingers felt
like steel bands, and she knew she had gone too
far.

'Perhaps you've only known boys, to be so auth-
oritative about them,' he drawled. 'A man is a different proposition altogether.'

As if she needed reminding! Her senses swam as
he filled her field of vision, her nostrils pulsating
with a mixture of outback scents blended with the
powerful male aroma he projected.

She tried to squirm away, but was held fast in
his iron grip. The kick she aimed at him glanced
off his elastic-sided boots. 'Let me go,' she insisted,
confused because he made her feel small and
helpless. It was an unaccustomed sensation, and she
wanted it to end.

'When you apologise. I've had it up to here with
your high and mighty attitude, Ms Richter.'

She tossed her head in a defiant gesture which
concealed her inner tremulousness. 'It takes one to
know one—*Mr McKinley*. If you weren't so sensitive about your masculinity, I wouldn't be here in
the first place. I should have remembered you're
touchy about it before I called you a boy. I
apologise for my memory lapse, but that's all.'

Fire danced in the black depths of his eyes. It
was like staring into leaping flames, and the heat
of it all but scorched her. 'My manhood isn't the
issue here. Your behaviour is.'

She searched her mind for a biting retort which would put him firmly in his place. She was a writer, for goodness' sake. Yet she couldn't think of a thing. His closeness seemed to have driven every coherent thought out of her head, replacing it with a maelstrom of sensations which roiled through her like a cyclone. 'It's a free country,' was the lamentable best she could do.

'Freedom confers responsibility as well as rights,' he reminded her. 'You may write what you please, but only if you're prepared for the consequences.'

'It's a fact of journalistic life that someone will always be unhappy with what I write. You can't please everyone.'

His gaze hardened. 'So you think what you did was justified?'

She felt the colour surge into her cheeks. 'It was an accident, a mistake.' Like coming out into the desert with him, she thought fleetingly. 'I am sorry those things I wrote about you got into print.'

'But not for writing them.'

He read the answer in her defiant gaze, even though her long lashes quickly veiled her response. 'So you do think I'm over-rated as a lover?'

'I was letting off steam when I wrote that. How should I know what sort of lover you are?'

The trap yawned widely, but not until she'd fallen headlong into it. He released one wrist and his hand wandered to the side of her face, his fingers caressing. 'There's one way to find out.'

His mouth found hers with unerring skill, his lips teasing and demanding all at once. His arm came around her shoulders, drawing her closer until she

was pressed against him, achingly aware of every
male curve and sinew outlined against her.

Something new and indefinable erupted through
her. So raw and unexpected was the feeling that her
will to resist vanished in an explosion of need such
as she had never known before.

As a child, she had burned her hand on a stove,
and recalled looking at the burn mark in fasci-
nation. Moments later, the pain had caught up,
searing her to her core. Bryan's kiss felt the same:
fascinating at first, then shocking as she realised
she was still playing with fire.

He was cast in the same mould as David Hockey.
Ruthless, taking what he wanted from life. Hadn't
she learned anything from her experience?

All the same, passion warred with common sense
as he deepened the kiss. Involuntarily her lips
parted, allowing him entry to the moist cavern of
her mouth. An electric charge jolted through her
as his teeth ground against her lower lip. His unshaven skin rasped against her cheek.

When had her arms crept up around his neck?
Pity help her, she was actually cupping the back of
his head to draw him closer. She dropped her hands
and twisted her head to one side, groaning as his
lips found the tender skin of her throat while his
absurdly long lashes feathered across her mouth.

'No, please,' she whimpered, the words as much
for herself as for him. She didn't want to be aware
of him as a man. She was here against her will, and
the sooner she returned to her own well-ordered life,
the better. This tide of erotic longings holding her
in thrall was a mistake. It had to be.

He finally allowed her to slide free, and she ran to the billabong to splash cool water over her burning face. Behind her, he laughed coldly. 'Next time, it may be simpler to apologise.'

She spun around, her face on fire. 'You're the one who should apologise for taking advantage of me when we're alone out here.'

'Taking advantage implies that it was one-sided. We both know it wasn't.'

It was futile to argue. She had already betrayed herself too thoroughly. Why was something she'd have to study more closely when she was alone. For now, attack seemed like the best form of defence. 'This is all about your male ego, isn't it?' she demanded, hurrying on before he could answer. 'Your male pride was wounded by my column, so your revenge is to seduce me. Then I'll have to admit I was wrong to cast aspersions on your skills as a lover. I'll bet you even made up the public relations job to get me into your clutches.'

She was shouting now, but she didn't care. Who would hear her besides the kangaroos and the dingoes? 'Well, why don't I save us both a lot of bother and admit it now? I was wrong and you're Australia's greatest lover. There, I've said it. Can I go back to Wildhaven now?'

'Have you finished?'

His question caught her by surprise. Hadn't he heard a word of her outburst? 'Your column made me well aware of what you think of me—or, should I say, how little,' he went on, 'but this has nothing to do with my ego, although it may have a lot to do with yours. Something about protesting too much, I believe.'

He brushed the back of his hand across his mouth
in a gesture which caused her stomach muscles to
cramp in response. The feel of his mouth was too
vividly imprinted on her mind. 'If I needed confirmation of how I can turn a woman on, you provided it most effectively just now. Would you care
for a repeat demonstration?'

He took a half-step towards her, and she retreated until she felt the hard bulk of the jeep at
her back. He hadn't moved any further, but she
had proved his point. 'Damn you,' she seethed.
'Hell will freeze over before I let you near me again
in this lifetime.'

A shiver shook her as his gaze dismissed her brave
denial for the lie it was. At the same time, a thrill
coursed through her, confusing in its intensity.
What was going on here? She hated him, yet every
move he made resonated through her like the
plucking of a harp string.

He frowned. 'No matter what you think of me,
I've never forced myself on a woman yet. And I
hate to disappoint you, but I didn't bring you out
here to seduce you. Bowana needs you, and that's
where you're going.'

'Then there really is a public relations job?' She
flinched as her voice came out infuriatingly husky.

He gave a sigh, but whether of regret or impatience she couldn't decide. 'Yes, there is. I'm
sorry if it shatters your illusions about being
dragged off to my harem.'

She drew herself up to her full height, which was
still only as far as his shoulder. 'Thanks, but I prefer
the job anyway.'

His mocking laughter followed her back to her car. 'You have a hell of a way of showing it, lady.'

He was whistling as he climbed aboard his jeep and gunned the motor. Damn the man. Why couldn't he accept her apology and let her go? He was obviously rich enough to hire anyone he wanted to solve his town's problems. Unless he believed in an eye for an eye. It would explain why only her personal service would satisfy his need for revenge.

The rough track demanded all her concentration as they continued on between crumbling sandstone cliffs and stands of tall gum trees. After a while the driving became automatic and her thoughts drifted back to the billabong. Kissing her had been an act of revenge, she was sure. Yet part of her had enjoyed surrendering to his embrace, and he knew it. How he must be laughing at her now.

Bryan McKinley and David Hockey were two of a kind, she reminded herself. They were both arrogant men who used their considerable charm to get what they wanted. Well, it had worked for David, but never again. Bryan had caught her off guard this time. Next time . . . no, there wouldn't be a next time, she vowed.

They stopped for lunch at a small freshwater spring. On the eastern bank were the remains of a rock wall built hundreds of years ago by local Aborigines. With maddening good humour, he ignored her deliberate coolness towards him and pointed out small gates in the rock walls. 'They allowed kangaroos and wallabies to reach the water to drink, where they made easy prey for the hunters.'

'A method you're familiar with, no doubt,' she murmured savagely.

He caught her wrist and swung her around. 'Wrong again. I'm a firm believer in the sporting chance.'

She looked disdainfully at the strong fingers looped around her wrist. The controlled strength in his grip amazed her anew. 'You mean the main chance, don't you?'

He released her and turned to the billy boiling on the open fire, tossing a handful of tea-leaves into it before he answered. 'If I did, you'd have a lot more to worry about than driving in the desert.'

She folded her arms across her body in an unconsciously defensive gesture. 'I'm sure they have laws about rape even in the desert.'

Hunkered down on the sand, he splashed tea into a pair of weathered enamel mugs and looked up at her, his eyes flashing a challenge. 'I wasn't talking about rape. I was thinking more along the lines of seduction.'

Alarm bells jangled in her head. She wished he wouldn't say such outrageous things while looking so heart-stoppingly masculine. It only confused the issue. 'I thought you said you weren't interested in seducing me.'

In one smooth movement, he rose and moved closer, but it was only to hand her one of the steaming mugs. 'I didn't say I wasn't interested, only that it wasn't the reason I brought you here.'

The tea she swallowed hastily scalded her throat, but she pretended enjoyment. Anything to disguise the confusion which roiled through her. She would be mad to encourage any such thing. On an outback property, the boss's word was law, and he had been a boss too long for his own good. She could imagine what sort of lover he would make—bold, demanding and probably insatiable. Giving pleasure would probably come a poor second to taking it.

She felt her colour heighten as her thoughts bolted like a wild horse. What on earth was she doing, thinking such things? It was precisely what he wanted her to think, she realised as he regarded her with wry amusement. 'Stop it,' she spluttered in fury.

He took a sip of his tea, his eyes assessing over the rim of his mug. 'Stop what?'

His innocent act didn't fool her for an instant. 'You know perfectly well. But I'm not—not interested.'

'Is there a man back in Perth?'

'I'm sure you know the answer already.' He was the one who'd had her investigated. Let him supply his own answers.

'I drew the line at bugging your bedroom,' he supplied mildly.

She rolled her eyes heavenwards. 'Thanks for small mercies.'

'But you haven't been seen with a new man for weeks. Are you still pining for David Hockey?'

Her mouth tightened. 'There's no point now I know he's still married.'

'But it did hurt?'

'Of course it did. What do you think I'm made of—stone?' It had hurt worse than she was willing to let him see. She had cried for two days after learning the truth, until she had convinced herself that he wasn't worth it. But even now, driving down his street was a bittersweet experience. Part of her innocence had been lost along with David, even though she no longer loved him. How could Bryan think she could escape with no scars?

His taunting look roved over her trim figure, outlined in designer jeans tucked into western-style boots. A man's checked shirt sculpted her full breasts and was tied at the waist for coolness. The top buttons were open, hinting at an expanse of cleavage which was probably more enticing than a low-cut blouse would have been. 'Stone is the last word I'd use to describe you. Pliant, yielding, deliciously soft...'

'But with a core of steel,' she snapped.

'Obviously I didn't hold you long enough to reach that part.'

'You can live in hope,' she said in a discouraging tone.

His eyes flashed. 'Is that a promise?'

The thought of his muscular arms closing around her drove out the clever retort she knew she ought to make. Whatever she said, he was determined to read what he liked into it. If this was his way of extracting revenge, it was masterly.

In her column, which had never been meant to see the light of day, if only she could make him believe it, she had called him an over-rated lover. Now he was making her eat those words.

No matter how he denied bringing her out here to seduce her, he was doing it with every word and gesture. She swallowed as her throat dried. Knowing what he was doing should have made her immune to him. But it only seemed to make her more aware of him as a man.

She looked desperately around them. 'Isn't the Canning stock route not far from here?'

He ran a finger across his lower lip, removing a last droplet of tea. He seemed well aware of her attempt to change the subject, and she wondered if he was going to let her get away with it. Then he relented. 'Yes, it is. This track is an offshoot of the main stock route which the surveyor Alfred Canning pioneered at the turn of the century.'

She gestured around them. 'Why would anyone in their right mind want to drive cattle through the western desert? It must be some of the most remote country on earth.'

'They had no choice. A cattle tick was plaguing the herds in the East Kimberley region. To stop it spreading, the farmers were banned from bringing their cattle into other parts of the state. They had to find other markets for their stock, which meant taking them overland through the desert, where the ticks couldn't survive.'

The thought of stockmen on horseback driving herds of cattle through this parched region was bleak. 'It must have been hell.'

He pushed his hat far back on his head. 'It was. Moving from sun up to sundown. Night watch till sunrise. Many of the Aboriginal stockmen did it just for their food and a blanket. On the way, I'll show you some of the wells which were built along the route to water the cattle.'

'I'd like to see them.' The change in his demeanour puzzled her. Apparently his arrogance didn't extend to this country or its traditional inhabitants, but only to her. He was a strange mixture, this Bryan McKinley.

CHAPTER FOUR

THE track to the well was clearly defined. Obviously the historical monument attracted the tourists, who braved the remote track in their four-wheel-drive vehicles.

Jill didn't know what she expected, but it wasn't the sturdy structure which greeted them. Much of the fencing was intact, and the well contained sweet water. Around it were stands of acacia, beefwood and mulga trees.

'It's beautiful,' she said. After staring at the blood-red sand for hours, this green oasis was heavenly.

He nodded. 'Whatever time of year I come here, it's always green.'

She gave him a speculative look. Out here he seemed more relaxed and outgoing somehow. 'We passed a lot of cattle on the way in. Who do they belong to?' she asked.

'The Canning stock route is a right of way and crosses a number of cattle stations, mine among them. Stock and horses from all of them drink at these wells.'

'And the saucer-shaped tracks I keep seeing in the sand? What makes them?'

He smiled tolerantly, and the transformation in his face was astonishing. It was just as well he didn't do it more often, Jill decided. It threw her completely off balance. 'They're made by wild camels,'

he explained. 'They're the survivors of the early
expeditions which opened up this country. Water
hauled up from the wells using camel power was
called ''whipping water''.'

She grimaced. 'They used to beat the poor animals to make them haul up the water?'

He shook his head. 'The camel walked back and
forth to raise and lower a bucket. It was suspended
on a pulley mounted on a whip pole over the well.'

Her smile was self-deprecating. 'I suppose it
doesn't pay to be too soft-hearted out here.'

'It's tough country, often deadly, and it breeds
tough people,' he agreed. 'But you'll also find some
of the biggest hearts in the outback.'

Thinking of him, she agreed with the tough part.
It was harder to imagine him as big-hearted when
she had yet to see proof that he owned such an
organ.

If he had, he would see that she didn't belong
here. She was hot, gritty, longing for a cool shower,
and felt as if she would explode if they drove over
yet another sand dune. It was humiliating to have
Bryan get out and push her vehicle when she stalled
before the top of a dune.

'The trick is to charge at the dune then quickly
change down the gears as you slow down on the
slope,' he advised with ill-disguised impatience.

Her eyes stung. 'It wouldn't be necessary if there
was a decent road in this place.'

Although her temper was frayed, he seemed un-
affected by the arduous hours on the road. His only
response was to hand her a mug of water from
the cooler in his jeep. 'Drink this. It may improve
your temper.'

'The only thing which will improve it is a trip back to Perth,' she snapped, but accepted the water. Obviously he wasn't about to let her die of thirst.

'Your love of the outback is touching,' he observed.

His sarcasm fuelled her anger. 'If you must know, I grew up in the outback. My father was a country policeman, retired now. I spent my childhood in places like Broome and Halls Creek, wherever he was posted.'

'But you couldn't wait to move to the city,' he guessed correctly from the derision in her voice.

She handed him the mug. 'Can you blame me? It got very wearing, always being the new kid at school, and making friends only to leave them behind whenever Dad was transferred.'

'So you stopped trying to make them,' he deduced with swift accuracy.

This was ground she preferred not to cover, especially not with him. 'Maybe I'd just had enough of heat, dust and flies. I gather you feel no such urge to stray.'

'I was born here, at Bowan Run, my family's original property outside Bowana,' he said, his tone provocative.

A swift flash of jealousy for his sense of belonging was overtaken by annoyance. 'How nice for you to have Daddy's company to inherit.'

A muscle worked in his jaw, betraying his quick flaring of anger. 'There was no silver spoon in my mouth,' he denied in a voice as cold as steel. 'Bowan Run was heavily mortgaged and run down when I took it over. My father had a heart condition which prevented him from doing much to keep it going.'

It was the opposite of what she had expected to hear, and it unsettled her to be wrong about him on this, at least. 'My mistake,' she murmured.

'I'll add it to my collection,' he rejoined drily. 'Fortunately my parents will be spared your barbed comments. They live in retirement in Darwin with my sister and her children.'

'Like my folks,' she surprised herself by volunteering. 'They live with our younger sister in Broome. I'm always hearing about the joys of married life.'

'More cynicism, Jill?'

'No, realism,' she fired back. 'My life suits me as it is, and I don't see why I should change it to please some man.'

Her chin lifted, defying him to fault her reasoning, hiding a truth she had only recently begun to face herself. As a result of her disjointed childhood, she not only avoided close friendships, but love as well. She still wasn't certain whether David's appeal had been because she had known instinctively that he was unavailable. She hated to admit it, but part of her had even been relieved to discover the truth.

'Then all I can say is, you haven't been in love,' Bryan said, homing in on her thoughts with unnerving accuracy.

Her eyebrows arched upwards. 'How would you know?'

'Because if you had, nothing else would matter.'

She shook her head, the dust-speckled curtain of hair flying around her head. 'You're wrong. My mother loved my father, but even she was worn down by the endless moving and resettling. It *does* matter, believe me. I vowed that when I grew up I would put down roots in the city and never set foot in the outback again.'

'Yet here you are.'

'Yes, here I am, hating every minute of it.'

His narrow-eyed scrutiny transfixed her. 'Are you quite sure you hate it so much? People change, you know.'

Her eyes flared a denial. 'Well, not me. Heat, dust and loneliness are what I remember most from my childhood, and they haven't changed.' Nor had the kind of man who tamed this forbidding land, she thought inwardly, her resentment growing.

'You can be just as lonely in the city as in the outback, sometimes more so,' he pointed out.

Unwillingly she recalled parties where she'd felt totally isolated, even though surrounded by dozens of people. Contrarily, she felt moved to defend her lifestyle. 'It isn't the same. Out here you can die without anyone knowing or caring.'

'You're wrong about the caring part. The outback was built on heroism and self-sacrifice.'

'Well, you're welcome to it,' she retorted, beyond minding. His enquiries were touching sensitive areas she preferred to leave unexplored. All she wanted was for this drive to end. If his town didn't have running water and electricity she would kill him.

He gestured impatiently. 'From now on you'll keep those views to yourself. We'll be in Bowana by sundown.'

Then he took her to visit the well, one of a string established by Canning when he had surveyed the stock route in 1908. Later visitors had maintained and restored the wells. The sight of the green oasis with its long history had restored some of her flagging spirits. She was in a much better mood by the time they set off to cover the remaining distance to the town.

As Bryan had promised, they arrived as the last rays of the sun were painting the town orange-gold. Many of the buildings were made of mud-brick and sandstone and dated back to the late 1800s.

The main street was easy to identify. It was the widest street, with a single-storeyed hotel, sandstone public administration building, a rambling general store, butcher's shop and very little else.

The surrounding cottages also looked original, with charming bull-nosed iron verandas and tumbledown outbuildings. A kelpie cattledog barked half-heartedly as they drove past.

Apprehension prickled through her. The town was smaller than the places to which her father had been posted. Putting Bowana on the map wasn't a challenge. It was mission impossible.

She cheered up a little when Bryan turned into the driveway of an imposing residence with wide verandas on three sides, supported by posts and embellished with complex fretwork. At least this house looked as if it ran to indoor plumbing.

'Your place?' she asked when they were parked in the wide gravel driveway.

He nodded. 'I can run things better from here than living on any one of the properties. They each have a resident manager, so they don't need another boss confusing the men.'

She studied the early Australian architecture. 'I didn't expect to find anything so imposing out here.'

He started to heave belongings out of the jeep.
'It was built for the resident magistrate of the
Bowana gold-fields, who was one of my forebears.
He worked his way up from inspector of police in
Derby to resident magistrate at Halls Creek, before
being transferred here.'

'He had good taste.'

As Bryan led the way inside, she was even more
impressed. The stone walls were immensely thick
and the tall windows were shuttered to keep out the
heat. She recognised a ventilated roof lantern as
typical of gold-fields buildings.

Doors opened off a wide hallway into spacious
rooms which felt blissfully cool after the heat of
the desert. She couldn't help admiring the pressed
metal ceilings. They were so intricate that they
wouldn't have looked out of place in a French
château.

He noticed her upward glance. 'Wait till you see
the one in the living-room. It's painted in thirty-
nine colours and embossed with eighteen-carat gold
leaf. Your bedroom ceiling has five hundred indi-
vidually hand-painted flowers.'

Her steps faltered. 'I beg your pardon?'

He nodded. 'I know because I counted them
when I was a kid, visiting my grandfather here.'

'I didn't mean the flowers. I meant the bit about
my bedroom. I thought I'd freshen up here, then
go on to the hotel for the night.'

'You wouldn't care for the Royal Hotel. It's not
a fit place for you to stay. It's far less regal than
its name suggests.'

As far as she knew, every town in Australia possessed at least one 'royal' hotel. In Australia, such

hotels were primarily drinking places, providing token accommodation at best. She shuddered, imagining what it would be like. 'All the same, I can't stay here with you.'

'Not decent?' He recalled their conversation on the track. 'You needn't worry. The guest quarters are self-contained and perfectly respectable.'

She would still be sharing a house with him, but there didn't seem to be much alternative. She could hardly turn around and drive back to Wildhaven, as well he knew. 'You might have warned me,' she said, trying for defiance and finding only weariness. Her doctor would be horrified if he knew how she'd spent her day. It hardly fitted her prescription of rest and relaxation.

He was unperturbed by her anger. 'I want you where I can keep an eye on you, which shouldn't come as any surprise. Your room is this way.'

Jill's shoulders drooped with tiredness as she followed him through the rambling old house. She'd been functioning on adrenalin all day, and the strain had caught up the moment she brought her car to a halt. All she wanted now was a wash and a long rest. They could argue over accommodation later.

As her footsteps dragged, Bryan turned to her, his expression irritated. 'I didn't think you were the type to sulk, Jill. It must have been obvious that accommodation here would be limited at best.'

How could he look so fresh and energised? Apart from a dusting of desert sand which made him look infuriatingly craggy and handsome, there was nothing to suggest he'd been on the road since sunrise.

For her part, she felt as if she'd run a marathon. Her skin felt gritty and hot, and strands of hair kept getting into her eyes. She pushed them away impatiently. 'It will be interesting to see what you tell the tourists you intend to bring here, when they find there's nowhere to stay.'

Annoyance gleamed in his dark gaze. 'The original plan was to offer farm-stay accommodation on the surrounding properties, to give visitors a taste of the real outback. I thought you'd be more comfortable staying in town.'

The implication was clear. He thought she was too spoiled to stay on a property, and her attitude now was bearing him out. His opinion of her shouldn't matter, but somehow it did. Should she tell him the real reason why she was on leave? He would have little sympathy for her illness, probably blaming it on her lifestyle, if he even believed her. She decided to keep her problems to herself.

'I'll be fine once I've had a shower,' she assured him, her voice vibrant with a tiredness which felt bone-deep. 'I'm not used to the heat.'

His eyes raked her, his expression scornful. 'This "Lady of the Camellias" act is a bit sudden, isn't it? You weren't bothered by the heat at Wildhaven.'

Her brother's house was air-conditioned and her workload entirely optional, but to say so would mean explaining about her state of health, and she didn't feel up to it right now.

Her chin came up, although she was aware of the infuriating sparkle of tears in her eyes. She blinked them away. 'I wasn't aware it was a crime to be tired.'

His set expression eased a little. 'You're right; it isn't. It's been a long day for both of us.'

She was amazed to hear him admit it. Surely he hadn't been as disturbed by her company as she was by his? As he manhandled her luggage through the doorway, she studied him covertly.

He looked anything but tired, yet his expression was wary, as if the day hadn't turned out quite as he expected. Kissing her at the billabong had been an act of revenge, even though her senses ran riot at the very thought. It was hard to believe it could have had an equally devastating effect on him.

There was no sign of it as he stepped aside to allow her to precede him into the room. Only his thoughtful gaze resting on her gave her pause. 'You should find everything you need here.'

Immediately she was conscious of a tension between them which hadn't existed a moment before. It throbbed between them like chords played by an unseen orchestra, the rippling notes seeming to draw them closer together.

She had taken a half-step towards him before she realised what she was doing and drew herself up. 'This will be fine, I'm sure.'

The room was as character-filled as the rest of the house. An antique lace spread covered a Queen Anne bed which looked large enough for two. Her eyes snapped away from it, focusing instead on the view of the front gardens from the French windows. A working fireplace had pride of place along another wall.

'Your bathroom is through here.' Bryan opened a door through which she glimpsed attractive period-style fixtures. The bath looked wonderfully

deep and reminded her of the weariness she hoped
to assuage in its depths.

'Are there any water restrictions?' she asked, remembering her childhood discipline. Water had
always been precious in the country towns where
she grew up. During droughts it was often rationed.

He shook his head. 'We have our own bore
supply and rainwater tanks as back-up, so there's
no need to limit yourself. Use as much as you like.'

It was an effort not to fling her arms around his
neck to show her gratitude. Only the thought that
if she did she might not want to let go held her
back. It was crazy, this longing to feel his arms
around her. It must be another symptom of the
virus. Her emotions were usually much better controlled. At least she'd learned something from her
experience with David Hockey. 'Thanks,' she said
weakly, aware that her legs weren't going to support
her for much longer. 'I'd like to try that bath now,'
she said in a maddeningly husky voice.

He seemed to snap out of whatever mood held
him in thrall. 'Fine. I'll finish unloading the cars.
We normally eat around seven.'

Who was we? she wondered, but he was gone
before she could ask. She'd find out soon enough.
For now, all she wanted was to fill that divine tub
with tepid water and soak her aches away.

The rest of her gear was standing near her
bedroom door when she emerged, pink and glowing
from her ablutions. She still felt bone-weary, but
less inclined to collapse at any moment. She was
towelling her hair dry when there was a knock at
her door.

Conscious that she was naked beneath the terry towelling robe she'd found in the bathroom, she eased the door open cautiously. Instead of Bryan, her caller was a stunningly beautiful young woman.

Taller than Jill, she was model-slender with spun gold hair which cascaded to her shoulders. Her hourglass figure reminded Jill of the cover girls hired by her magazine.

'Yes?' she queried, feeling at a decided disadvantage.

The woman slid around Jill and into the room. 'Hello, I'm Christa Bernard. Bryan and I live together.'

It was the last thing Jill had expected to hear. With an almost physical sense of shock, she spun back into the room, clutching the robe around her in an instinctively defensive gesture. 'You mean you're Bryan's housekeeper,' she managed to amend.

The other woman lowered her eyes. 'You could put it that way, country morality being what it is.' Her coquettish smile implied a sisterly sharing of the truth, which for some reason made Jill feel as if her heart had suddenly skipped a beat.

Tiredness and surprise had to explain the re-action, she thought as her thoughts raced chaotically. She could hardly believe that Bryan lived with this stunning-looking woman.

He lived with her.

After preaching to Jill about her supposed lack of morals, how could he have kissed her with such fervour, knowing that Christa waited for him at home?

Distantly she heard herself exchanging pleasantries. Beneath the surface, Jill struggled to make sense of Bryan's behaviour towards her. What a hypocrite he was, lecturing her about David when he lived his own life as he chose.

It was only when Christa left her to prepare dinner that Jill had time to wonder why his behaviour was any concern of hers.

CHAPTER FIVE

THE fact that Bryan McKinley was living with someone didn't bother her in the least. Or so Jill tried to tell herself as she slammed a book down so hard that dust rose in a cloud. The motes danced in the sunlight streaming through the French doors. Some journalist she was, not to have uncovered the fact for herself when she researched his background for the column.

She suppressed a sneeze. Didn't Bryan ever dust his library? It was hard enough wading through these old tomes in search of a brilliant idea, without having to endure a century of accumulated dust as well.

Face it, the books aren't the problem; Christa Bernard is, she admitted to herself. Against all common sense she had been shaken by Christa's presence, since Bryan hadn't so much as hinted at a serious involvement. The thoroughness with which he had kissed Jill had suggested the opposite.

It wasn't as if Jill cared what he did. He could live with triplets for all it mattered to her. It was more the principle of the thing. Men who were spoken for should keep their hands to themselves.

Typical, she harumphed, tugging another book down from the shelf and flicking through it. Men like David Hockey and Bryan McKinley had no principles. Women were playthings to them. What the lady didn't know wouldn't hurt her.

Well, it did hurt, sooner or later. But she had learned her lesson. Christa could have Bryan and she was welcome to him.

Hefting a small black rock which had pride of place on one shelf, she was torn by a sudden urge to hurl it through the nearest window. Hastily replacing the rock, she searched her conscience. She wasn't protesting too much where Bryan was concerned, was she? It was the shock of discovering he was as bad as David Hockey which made her want to throw things, not any feelings she harboured for the man himself. She refused to accept any other explanation.

'Ready for some coffee?'

She looked up as Christa came in, balancing a tray. 'You shouldn't wait on me. I'm here to work.'

Christa put the tray down and handed Jill a cup, black and strong, the way she preferred it. Homemade Anzac biscuits sat beside it. 'You are so single-minded about your work. I could never give myself up to a career the way you do.'

'You work with Bryan,' Jill reminded her around a mouthful of biscuit. It galled her to admit it, but Christa was a brilliant cook. Her dishes had managed to perk up even Jill's jaded appetite. Bryan also ate her sumptuous meals with every sign of enjoyment, she noticed.

'That's different. In the outback it's taken for granted that a woman works alongside her man, looking after his house and children, and helping on the land.'

Jill's mouth twisted ironically. 'You don't call that work? You probably put in a longer day than I do at the magazine.'

A glint of triumph lit Christa's eyes as she snapped her fingers. 'I knew I'd heard your name before somewhere. You're *that* Jill Richter, the one who wrote all those wicked things about Bryan, aren't you?'

'I'm afraid so,' Jill admitted. 'The column was a joke, not meant to get into print. The magazine ran it by accident while I was ... while I was away.'

'He was mad as hell when I showed him my copy,' Christa said, sounding almost pleased about it. 'Imagine calling Bryan over-rated as a lover.'

Her wistful smile was meant to convey intimate knowledge of the facts, Jill gathered. Her anger rose, although it was as much at herself as at Bryan.

How could she have wasted a minute imagining herself in his arms? She ought to have known there would be a woman in his life. *He* should have let her know, she fumed inwardly. Just like David Hockey, he had preferred to indulge his whims, conveniently overlooking the woman waiting for him at home.

'You'd know better than me,' she said, managing to sound world weary and uninterested at the same time. 'As you just observed, my heart is in my work.'

Christa contrived a giggle. 'So's mine. I'm glad we understand each other.'

Over Jill's shoulder, she glanced at the book which lay open on top of the growing pile. 'Find anything interesting yet?'

Jill shook her head. 'Nothing which would attract tourists to Bowana so far.'

'You won't find anything, either. It's a dry, dusty cattle town which died long ago but didn't have the sense to fall over.'

Astonishment darkened Jill's eyes. 'I thought you loved it here.'

'I love the life I can have with Bryan. If only he wasn't so unyielding, he'd see that he can run his cattle empire from anywhere in the world. He doesn't need this dreary little town.'

'Then why is he trying so hard to save it?'

Christa shrugged. 'That same die-hard streak, I suppose. When the town fails, he'll have done all that was humanly possible for them.'

When it failed? Christa sounded as if she couldn't wait for it to happen. Bryan was unlikely to agree. This land was his birthright. His roots were here, his dreaming, as the Aboriginals called it. Didn't Christa realise that if Bowana died part of Bryan's spirit would die with it?

Anger flooded through her, so raw and unexpected that she caught her breath. If Christa really loved Bryan, she should support him in his quest, instead of praying for him to fail.

It was none of her business, she told herself fiercely. Steadying her breathing with an effort, she picked up the black rock and used it to gesture to the others displayed around the library. 'Who's the rock collector?'

Christa made a face. 'Not me. They're Bryan's old things. When we leave here, I'd like nothing better than to see them left behind.'

When they left here ... When they were married, perhaps ... Jill supplied the rest, and suppressed a fresh wave of annoyance. How could a marriage succeed when Christa clearly disliked everything which he held dear? She must have other attributes which compensated, Jill thought waspishly.

She had no trouble picturing him as a geologist. He and the land were one. Her hand tightened around the specimen, and some of its power seeped into her fingers. The blue-black colouring was an oddity in a country of blood-red earth, and the texture differed from the other rocks in the collection. Carefully, she returned it to its place. 'I'd better get back to work.'

Christa waved a hand at the books. 'I don't know why you bother. Practically our only claim to fame is the Bowana cattle trail, which used to link up with the Canning stock route.'

'Bryan explained about the Canning on the way here.' Jill sounded distracted as an idea leapt into her mind. 'You had your own branch of the stock route here?'

'It was only used a handful of times until the 1950s, mostly by the black stockmen. Nothing to get excited about.'

'Not to you, perhaps. But to city people who've never ridden with cattle before, it could be a fantasy come true.'

Why hadn't she thought of it straight away? Seeing the stock route with Bryan had fired her own imagination, so why not those of tourists who could ride the trail for themselves?

The Aboriginal people would need to be consulted, since the route probably crossed their land. They could share their dreamtime heritage with the visitors. Everyone would benefit. Her eyes gleamed with excitement. 'It has to be the answer.'

'Sounds as if you two are on to something,' Bryan said, joining them in the library.

Involuntarily, Jill's heartbeat quickened at the sight of him, hot and dusty, but radiating a powerfully masculine aura which set her pulses racing. He had no right to stand there looking so attractive and so infuriatingly unavailable.

Her heart trip-hammered in her chest as his gaze swept from Christa to Jill. 'What's going on here?'

Jill opened her mouth to speak, but was forestalled by Christa. 'I was telling Jill about my idea to reopen the old Bowana stock trail to tourists. I wasn't sure if I should mention it, since Jill's the expert here, but she wasn't getting anywhere, so...'

She let her voice trail off on a note of feminine uncertainty. 'It has possibilities,' he confirmed thoughtfully. He ruffled Christa's hair with a gesture which evoked a savage response in Jill. 'What's your professional opinion, Jill?'

Anything Jill said now would sound like sour grapes, she thought grimly. Christa had neatly hijacked her idea without a glimmer of conscience, leaving Jill no option but to agree. 'Oh, it's a terrific idea,' she said, looking pointedly at Christa.

She didn't even blush. 'It's all yours, Jill. Marketing is for you slick city types. But you will make sure they print the right story, won't you?'

Jill seethed inwardly. In one breath, Christa had imbued her with all the perceived evils of the city and also reminded Bryan of the libellous column.

His expression hardened. 'Everyone's entitled to one mistake.' His frosty tone reminded Jill that she wouldn't be allowed a second one.

Christa smiled sweetly. 'Of course. I'm not saying she'd do to Bowana what she did to you, but we can't be too careful, can we?'

'You needn't worry. I have the situation well in hand.' His eyes were levelled at Jill, but he spoke to Christa. 'Don't you have a breeding programme to check on today?'

Christa pouted. 'If you say so.'

'I say so.' He patted her possessively on the rear as she headed for the door with obvious reluctance. 'Don't work too hard, Jill,' she said as she went out.

Jill stood up, her limbs rigid with anger. She'd had about enough of Christa's veiled comments. 'Since I'm so unreliable, maybe you two should handle this yourselves.'

Unperturbed, Bryan crossed his arms over his broad chest. 'Jealous, Jill?'

Her eyes flared. Did he know how she'd been imagining herself in Christa's place? That every time he touched the other woman Jill's senses ran riot, although she told herself it was insane? How could he possibly have guessed? 'Why should I be jealous?' she asked carefully.

'Because Christa had the bright idea of re-opening the cattle trail. If it gets you out of here all the sooner, I should think you'd be pleased.'

Jill's knees weakened. He thought she was jealous of Christa's *idea*. How insensitive could he be? 'Of course I'm not jealous,' she said dismissively. 'At work we brainstorm ideas all the time. It's what you do with the idea that matters. But if I'm to do anything with this idea, I'm going to need your trust and support.'

His lowered lashes veiled his dark eyes, making them unreadable. 'In the outback, trust is something you earn.'

And she hadn't earned his. Her spirits sank. How long was she to go on paying for one stupid mistake? At the same time, she acknowledged that the column could never have been published if she hadn't written it in a fit of childish pique.

Well, if trust had to be earned, she would darned well earn his and make him eat his words about her work being frivolous. 'Then the sooner I start developing this idea, the better, wouldn't you say?'

He lifted the books from her hands, set them down, then dusted her palms with his fingers. His touch was light but strangely erotic, as if he had kissed the sensitive skin instead of brushing it with his fingertips. She glanced at her hands, expecting to see some mark, and was mildly surprised to find none.

'The project can wait until after lunch,' he insisted. 'It's time you saw more of the town than this house.'

He was only taking her out as part of her education, but she couldn't suppress a thrill of anticipation. 'Where are we going?'

'Would you believe the Royal Hotel?'

'I thought you said it was a dump.'

His eyes sparkled. 'I told you it wasn't a fit place for you to stay. The rooms are basic but liveable for the stockmen and ringers who stay there. At lunchtime they serve the best barbecued steaks in the outback.'

A flush swept over her as he took her arm to escort her the short distance down the main street to the Royal Hotel. She told herself it was the afternoon heat which brought the colour rushing to her features. It had nothing to do with the touch of his hand on her bare forearm.

The Royal Hotel was an ageing dowager of a building, the hand-made bricks etched by years of sandstorms blowing in off the desert. Many bricks had initials chipped into them, most eroded with the passage of years. One set of initials was dated 1901.

Inside Jill blinked in the dimness, her eyes gradually adjusting to the shadowy interior of the hotel. A group of men—stockmen, judging by their clothes—propped up the main bar. Bryan was greeted cordially as he escorted her through the room to a room at the back.

She looked around with interest. The room had evidently been built later than the rest of the hotel. There were three walls of brick and a fourth of latticed timber, open to whatever cooling breezes could be coaxed inside. Enormous ceiling fans moved lazily overhead. It was like something out of *Casablanca*.

'The barbecue's over there. You choose your own steaks and Fred cooks them for you.' He indicated a vast black hotplate on which slabs of meat as big as dinner plates were sizzling.

'They're enormous,' she said with a slight shudder. Her appetite had suffered along with the rest of her health since her illness.

'You can have a chicken kebab if you prefer,' he informed her. 'But I recommend the steak. You need a bit of building up.'

'Thanks a lot. I worked hard for this shape,' she defended herself. As a result of the virus, she had lost more weight than was good for her, but it stung to have him point it out. She was sure he didn't make such patronising remarks to Christa.

He steered her to a corner table and drew out a chair for her. 'You work too hard. You don't have to solve all of Bowana's problems in a day, you know.'

'I thought that's what I'm here for.'

He folded his arms across the table and leaned closer. 'In Australia, there's city time and country time. Here, we work on country time. What isn't done today will get done tomorrow.'

'*Mañana, mañana,*' she said under her breath.

His fingers clamped around her wrist. 'Mock all you like, but it's a healthier lifestyle than yours, I'll be bound.'

Ironically, he was more right than he knew, but she wasn't about to admit it. He would only use her vulnerability against her if she gave him the chance.

'If your lifestyle is so idyllic, why do you need me to attract people to sample it?' she asked.

Sparks flew from the flinty black eyes. 'You never miss an opportunity, do you? No wonder it was left to Christa to come up with a workable idea. At least her heart's in the project.'

He obviously had no idea that Christa was only waiting for her chance to leave Bowana behind for good. There was no point in Jill trying to enlighten him. Christa would simply deny it, and it was obvious whose side he would take. It hadn't even occurred to him that the idea for the tourist cattle drive might be Jill's.

The distress which accompanied the thought caught her by surprise. It was crazy. She wasn't here by choice, so she shouldn't care if he didn't give her credit for her idea. Accepting praise from him would be like taking crumbs from his table. Surely she'd rather starve?

'You must be Jill.'

She started as a huge man loomed over their table and enveloped her hand in both of his. 'It's a pleasure to have you here.'

Bryan nodded to the new arrival. 'G'day, Fred. Jill, this is Fred Gardiner, the licensee of the Royal Hotel. Fred, the lady whose hand you're about to crush beyond recognition is Jill Richter.'

With a stammered apology, the big man released her hand, and she massaged her fingers unobtrusively. 'Hello, Fred. I'm pleased to meet you, too.'

He smiled, showing uneven white teeth. 'This is a great thing you're doing for us, Jill. I have two teenage boys and my sister has three kids under fifteen. If you can get the tourists to come to Bowana, maybe our kids won't have to move away to find work when they're older.'

She shifted uncomfortably, his praise sitting awkwardly with the real reason she was here—to satisfy Bryan's quest for revenge. How could he sit there so calmly, knowing she was here under false pretences? 'I haven't really done anything yet,' she evaded. 'This project is really Bryan's baby.' There, let him talk his way out of that.

Fred surprised her by nodding agreement. 'I should have known, after all he's done for us over the years. If anyone can make it work, he can.'

So much for her line about delusions of sainthood, she thought furiously. Around the town, he was obviously halfway towards canonisation already. She opened her mouth to say something, but was quickly forestalled by Bryan.

'This is a team effort, Fred. We're in this together.'

Fred glanced towards the steaks sizzling on the barbecue. 'Duty calls, but if there's anything I can do to help...'

'We'll call on you,' Bryan supplied.

The man returned to his work, flipping steaks and onion rings with a practised hand. Jill watched him thoughtfully. She didn't like the discovery that the town's problems had a human face. It complicated her desire to get out of here as soon as she decently could.

Bryan anticipated her thoughts. 'This town is full of folk like Fred. They built this country and they deserve to get something back for their children, whether you like the idea or not.'

'I have no difficulty with the idea, only with the way in which you achieve your goals,' she said tautly. She wondered what Christa thought of Bryan's feelings for the townspeople. It wasn't something he was likely to give up lightly, as Jill herself knew to her cost.

She was grateful for the excuse to get up and select her meal from the barbecue. It gave her the time to get her emotions back under control. However worthy Bryan's goals might be, they didn't excuse his methods. She still hadn't forgiven him for threatening her brother and sister-in-law.

Saint Bryan he might be to the people of Bowana, but to her he was still a sinner. Saints didn't blackmail people and they didn't mislead them with kisses when they were living with someone else.

Plate in hand, she froze halfway to the barbecue. What was going on here? Was her resentment directed at the way he'd dragged her out here against her will, or at him for kissing her when he was living with Christa? Reluctantly, she faced the possibility that there might be a much more personal reason for her feelings. She couldn't be attracted to him, woman to man, could she?

It must be the desert heat addling her brains, she told herself. A woman would have to be crazy to fall for such an arrogant, controlling man. Why, he didn't understand the meaning of the word 'no'.

She couldn't imagine pretending to have a headache if he wanted to make love. What he wanted, he would make sure she wanted, too. His dreams would be hers, his star the one he would expect his wife to follow.

'Steak or chicken, love?'

She snapped out of her reverie. What was she thinking of, entertaining such foolish notions? She was here to do a job, not to get involved with the last man on earth who should interest her.

She summoned a shaky smile for Fred. 'Chicken, thank you,' she replied, and wondered whether she was referring to the meal or herself.

CHAPTER SIX

BY THE time Jill returned to the table, leaving Fred in charge of cooking her meal, she was composed again, at least on the outside. Inside, she was more confused than ever.

It was obvious from the way Bryan was treated by the others in the dining-room that she was the only one with any reservations about him.

They didn't stop her heart from picking up speed as she approached his table. A shaft of sunlight spilled across it, catching him as if in a spotlight, and a lump rose in her throat.

His mouth was parted in a half-smile at something he was thinking. Recalling the pressure of that same mouth against hers made the plate of salad she carried tremble in her hands.

She put it down quickly and dropped into her seat before he could come around and pull her chair out for her. She found she needed the width of the table between them to tame her whirling thoughts.

'You didn't order anything,' she said, coughing to clear a dry throat.

He nodded towards the barbecue. 'Fred knows how I like my steak.'

A question rose in her mind. 'How did he know what I'm doing here?'

'It's a small community. News travels fast.'

'Do they also know I'm not exactly a volunteer?'

A warning light flickered in his eyes. 'I didn't see the need to pass along that particular detail.'

'It wouldn't exactly enhance your reputation, would it?' she snapped, disturbed by her growing tension. In the face of Fred's warmth, she felt like a fraud. This project meant much more to the townsfolk than she liked to think.

'My reputation doesn't matter,' he dismissed her taunt. 'You saw how much your presence here means. Would you like to be the one to disillusion Fred and his family?'

She looked down at her plate. 'No.'

'Neither would I.'

As she picked at her plate of salad, he gave a growl of impatience. Now what had she done wrong? He went to the bar and returned with slabs of home-made bread which he dumped on to her plate. 'You can't exist on rabbit food alone. Those shadows under your eyes could be mistaken for a solar eclipse.'

'I realise I'm no Christa Bernard, but you don't have to be insulting,' she said. She was tempted to push the bread away as a further act of defiance, but it smelled so mouth-watering that she couldn't bring herself to do it. Mechanically she began to butter a piece.

He looked startled. 'You think I'm comparing you to Christa?'

'And finding me wanting,' she said around a mouthful of the delicious bread.

'Hardly that, Jill. No man could look at you and find you wanting, as I'm sure you're well aware.' Unexpectedly, he cupped her chin and turned her to face her reflection in a mirror over the bar. 'What do you see when you look there?'

What she saw made her limbs feel weak. Her dark brown hair was haloed with light from the garden behind them. Her head was close to Bryan's, her chin caught in his fingers. They were so close together that the slightest turn would bring their mouths into alignment.

What was she thinking of? Only moments before they had been discussing Christa. Jill wrenched her head away. 'I see a fish out of water, if you must know.'

'Are you sure, Jill?'

'What does it matter anyway? I'm only here to do a job, not to fall in love with the town.' Or its charismatic leader, she added to herself.

She was reprieved by Fred calling them to collect their meals. Bryan got up to collect them, and by the time he returned she was composed again, at least outwardly.

'Will Christa be joining us later?' she asked doggedly, ignoring the pang which shot through her as she voiced the question.

He shook his head. 'She's gone to Bowan Run to check on a breeding programme I'm running there.'

Her surprise was quickly masked. 'I didn't realise that Christa was involved in your pastoral company. I thought she was mainly your housekeeper.'

He gave her a calculating look. 'I can imagine what you thought. But Christa can do the work of most men. As well as farm management, she rides, ropes and brands a calf with the best of them. It's a damned shame her older brother will inherit their family property, but her father's old-fashioned. He wants Christa to marry and live on her husband's place.'

From Christa's disparaging comments about the town, she was hardly likely to care if the land went to her brother, although she was wise enough not to betray herself to Bryan. And he thought city women were manipulative.

Jill vented some of her annoyance on the chicken kebab, prising the tender meat off the skewer with unnecessary vigour. It gave her some small satisfaction to be sure that Christa wouldn't find it easy to persuade Bryan to exchange his outback lifestyle for something more to her liking. He was the original immovable object.

There was no reason why it should concern Jill, but it did. Christa's wiles offended her. It had nothing to do with the attractiveness of the man sitting opposite her, eating his steak with quiet appreciation.

His stillness was one of his most appealing qualities, she realised. He could make silence seem companionable. Yet he was also the man who had blackmailed her into taking this job, she made herself remember. His threat to foreclose on her brother's mortgage still rankled. He and Christa probably deserved each other.

He put his cutlery down and reached for his beer glass. When he drained it, there was a rim of foam frosting his upper lip. She stared at it, mesmerised, until he skimmed it away with the back of a finger.

She swallowed tautly, forcing herself to bring the other woman back into the conversation. 'I suppose you and Christa grew up together.'

'Not really. We're neighbours, but the two homesteads were half a day's ride apart. We spoke on the radio through School of the Air, and met at social gatherings, but I didn't really get to know her until my father became seriously ill.'

His voice grew distant and his knuckles tightened around the empty beer glass. 'If it hadn't been for Bill Bernard, we'd have lost our land to the bank. Heaven knows how, but he kept our place going as well as his own when Dad was too sick to manage.'

'What about your mother?' she asked, recalling Christa's remark about outback women working alongside their menfolk.

His gaze softened. 'Mum did what she could, but she had her hands full caring for Dad.'

'So most of the hard work fell to you.'

'I couldn't have done it without Bill Bernard. When I found out he'd seen your column and been hurt by it, I could have cheerfully killed you.'

Now she understood why his vendetta was so personal, and a sharp pang of sorrow for her inadvertent action pierced her. She hadn't meant any of this to happen. Even if Bryan overestimated Bill's role in saving his property and underestimated his own, it was obvious he believed himself heavily indebted to the other man. To the point of marrying his daughter? She was surprised by the rush of feeling the question generated.

'And now you're the big boss of the McKinley Pastoral Company,' she said, unwilling to acknowledge that his story had impressed her. 'No doubt you enjoy throwing your weight around.'

'I use my authority when it's necessary,' he reminded her silkily. No doubt he included bringing her to Bowana among those times. 'Otherwise, the company runs smoothly with minimal intervention from me.'

'Yet you had no compunction in forcing me to do your bidding,' she couldn't help throwing at him. Attack seemed like the best form of defence, considering the rampant way her emotions were running as she faced him across the table.

His eyes slitted and his fingers closed over hers, inexorably drawing her closer to him. 'You're determined to see me as some kind of outback tyrant, aren't you? Well, so be it. I have no need to prove— or disprove—anything to you.'

His touch fired her senses, and it took all her resolve not to pull away until he saw fit to release her. Shakily, she reached for her sunhat. 'I should get back to my research.'

Overriding her feeble objections, he paid for lunch and they walked back to the house in tense silence. She was surprised when he followed her into the library.

'I'd like to hear more about this cattle trail idea,' he said, dropping into a winged leather chair.

Ignoring the prickling sense of awareness generated by his presence was an effort, but she managed it. 'Well, it's still no more than an idea, but people are always looking for novel holidays. What better than to ride in the footsteps of the pioneers on a real-life cattle drive?'

'Do you propose to use real cattle?'

Her enthusiasm grew. 'Why not? Experienced stockmen could supervise the tourists as well as a small herd. The more authentic the experience, the better.'

His frown of concentration deepened. 'You could be right. I don't suppose you're aware that many of the big properties are already returning to traditional means of mustering cattle?'

'I thought everything was done by motorbike and helicopter nowadays.'

'It was, but now horses are being brought back after nearly twenty years. Mustering by chopper is fast and efficient, but the pace inevitably sees calves separated from their mothers and the stock getting exhausted and over-heated.'

She felt her skin flush, but refused to consider that his approval had anything to do with the reaction. 'So you agree that the idea has merit?'

'Indeed, but it seems to need something more, something unique to this area.'

'I thought so, too.' She picked up the blackened stone and hefted it in her palm. 'I was wondering about this.'

He gave a wry smile. 'Your journalistic eye doesn't miss much. Do you have any idea what you're holding?'

'Some kind of geological specimen, obviously.'

'Much more. A piece of the moon.'

The fingers she'd curled around the rock flew open, and she gazed at the fragment in wide-eyed astonishment. 'You're not serious?'

'It's one of only a dozen lunar samples found on earth, brought here by meteorites. Most of the others were at the edges of the Antarctic. I had this one authenticated at a university lab in Arizona which handled samples from the Apollo moon missions, so it's the real McCoy.'

The sample seemed to glow in her palm, but she knew it was her runaway imagination at work. 'And you found it around here?'

He folded his arms across his broad chest and regarded her impatiently. 'This area is the meteorite capital of the world. My moon rock comes from Turuga, the largest McKinley station, where there's a meteorite crater wide enough to hold your cattle drive in.'

Excitement radiated through her. 'This is it. This is the answer to Bowana's problems.'

His expression became shuttered suddenly. 'If you're suggesting I should sell the lunar specimen, it's out of the question. It's worth far more to Australia's heritage than the million or so it would fetch in cash.'

Her eyes snapped with annoyance. 'I don't mean sell it. I mean exhibit it to attract people to the area. The Turuga crater would be the perfect focal point of the cattle drive, and this could be the drawcard.'

He cupped his chin between thumb and forefinger. 'It's good, damned good. We could house the meteorite collection in a museum in the town, for those who don't want to tackle the cattle drive. Either way, it brings tourists and work for the young people, so they don't have to move away. By Harry, it might work.'

A shriek was torn from her as his hands spanned her small waist. He swung her off the floor and around until she begged dizzily for release. Taking his time, he complied, and her body slid slowly against his as he lowered her to the floor.

The moment became electrified.

His eyes met hers in silent communion as he kept his hands around her. Tension flooded through her as she became aware of every hard contour of his body aligned with hers. He was breathing heavily, his heart beating a powerful tattoo against her chest. Her own pulses raced, recognising where she was, and how much she wanted to be here.

'Jill...' The rawness in his voice startled her, redolent with a passion and a need exceeding her own. It wasn't possible that he shared this exquisite, torturous sense of longing, was it?

'Yes,' she murmured, mindless of everything but the power and passion of his embrace.

A gasp escaped her as he slid a hand under her knees and swept her into his arms, carrying her to the Chesterfield sofa under the window, where he placed her with tender care.

Kneeling beside her, he ravaged her mouth with kisses, and she linked her arms around his neck, kissing him back with an abandonment which astonished her.

This was wrong. The thought echoed hollowly through her mind, just as swiftly overlaid by a desire so strong that she felt shaken. Against all common sense, she wanted him to kiss her as he was kissing her, to touch her in all her secret places as he was touching her. She wanted it so much that she was a quivering mass of needs to be moulded at his whim, to his heart's desire.

When he undid the buttons of her shirt she moaned with pleasure, because he could finally caress her breasts, which strained her bra. Her nipples felt so sensitised that she wanted to cry out when his fingers teased them.

'You're so beautiful,' he murmured, his lips moving against her throat so she felt his words as well as heard them. 'So beautiful.'

She arched against him, his breath fiery against her bared skin. His face was dark, his breathing fast and shallow, as if he, too, was as caught up in the moment as she was.

His other hand splayed across her hip, massaging the curve of her thigh with mind-tearing strokes. The hands she had instinctively pressed against his chest to ward him off had somehow entangled themselves in the silken strands of his hair. One slid down the column of his neck, the faint furring of hair unbelievably erotic as it grazed her palm.

'Yes, my darling, yes,' she breathed, hardly aware of having voiced the thought until she felt him unfasten her jeans.

The denim flared wide, exposing the frivolous black lace beneath. Her weakness for lacy underthings had made her the butt of family jokes since her teens, but now she was glad to be wearing something so glamorous when she saw the gleam of interest in Bryan's eyes.

He ran a finger around the lacy band riding low across her flat stomach. 'How did you know I liked black lace?'

Wave after wave of sensation ripped through her as he traced a pattern across her stomach with his fingers. She could hardly speak for the anticipation which had almost closed her throat. 'Do you?' she asked in a hoarse, emotion-clogged whisper.

He traced the flowery pattern all the way to where it disappeared under stonewashed denim. 'Yes, but not as much as what it conceals.'

Distantly, alarm bells rang in her head as she struggled to remember where and who they were. This wasn't supposed to be happening. Yet, cradled across his lap, she felt his hardening desire for her, and her own body melted in instinctive response.

When he lowered his head and rained kisses on the cleft between her breasts she arched against him helplessly, her mind emptying of all coherent thought except the need to be one with him.

As he drank his fill of her breasts, sensation slammed through her with a force which left her breathless. A fire-storm started in the core of her being, until she wondered how anyone could live through such sweet torment.

'Love me, please, Bryan,' she moaned, her eyes closing against the field of stars filling her vision.

'No.'

With a roar of anger, he wrenched himself away from her and went to the window, slamming his open palm against the window-ledge with a force which rattled the panes.

He looked as if he had just run a particularly gruelling race. His clothes were in disarray and his hair was tousled where she'd run her fingers through it. Yet all the passion had drained from his expression, leaving a cold anger which struck at her heart.

Despite the heat, she felt icy without his arms around her. 'What is it? What's wrong?' she asked, her voice reedy with uncertainty.

'You know perfectly well what's wrong,' he ground out, separating each word so it sounded like an accusation.

'No, I don't. Tell me.'

With slow, deliberate movements, he slid his shirt back into his trousers and thrust his hair back, using his fingers as a comb. 'To think I almost fell for this new ploy of yours. What a fool you must think I am.'

She felt as if the world were shifting beneath her feet. 'What ploy? I haven't the faintest idea what you're talking about.'

His hard gaze raked her. 'Haven't you, Jill? Then this isn't a new version of "get Bryan McKinley"?'

'Of course it isn't. I shouldn't have let you make love to me, knowing what you think of me. But it wasn't part of any plot. You make me sound like some kind of Lorelei, luring men to their fates.'

'Aren't you? David Hockey probably thinks you are.'

'This wasn't all my fault,' she defended herself, hurt beyond measure that he should think there was some kind of ulterior motive behind her actions.

'Granted, and I don't absolve myself for one minute. You're a damnably attractive woman, Jill. You could tempt any man beyond human endurance.'

'Then why treat me like a criminal? Couldn't the same thing have happened to me?'

'Not with your track record.'

Her blood ran hot with unfulfilled desires, to which was added anger at the unfairness of this. Just because she had unwittingly been involved with a married man—whom she'd dropped as soon as she discovered the truth—Bryan was determined to see her as some sort of scarlet woman. 'You're wrong about me,' she said with all the dignity she could muster.

His eyes were hooded. With the light from the window behind him, he looked dark and avenging. His voice reached her from the depths of the shadows. 'Am I? Then tell me you didn't know that Christa and I are engaged to be married.'

CHAPTER SEVEN

IT WAS one thing to suspect that Christa wanted Bryan to marry her, but quite another to hear him confirm it.

Jill felt numb as she fastened her shirt with trembling fingers. Her skin was cold where only minutes before it had burned with the fire of his touch.

Stiffly swinging her legs to the floor, she hunched her shoulders as if to protect herself from the onslaught of his accusations. How could she have allowed herself to be swept away by his caresses when Christa's shadow lay over them the whole time? It was like David all over again. She couldn't believe it was happening to her a second time.

This was different, she acknowledged in growing despair. She had cared for David, but had never yearned for his touch the way she craved Bryan's. His high-handed behaviour towards her made it hard even to like him, but it didn't stop her senses from leaping into overdrive the moment he entered a room.

'So it's true,' she said dully.

He swivelled, his look searing her. 'Then you admit it; you did know?'

The censure in his gaze made her flinch. 'Despite what you think, this isn't some game. I don't want to come between you and Christa. She suggested there was something between the two of you, but I didn't know you were officially engaged.'

'As it happens, it isn't official, but we do have an understanding,' he told her coldly. 'If you had known, would it have made a difference?'

Shocked by the accusation buried in his question, she jolted upright. 'Of course it would have. I was shattered when I found out that David was still married. I vowed never to let such a thing happen to me ever again.'

Her voice cracked as she relived the pain of finding out that not only was David still married, but he had every intention of remaining so. Bryan's accusation had reopened the scarcely healed wounds, adding fresh scars of his own which would take even longer to repair.

'Well, I'm glad your conscience is clear,' he said harshly, 'because mine isn't.'

It was far from clear, she realised with a pang. Any scruples she owned had fled the moment his hands took possession of her breasts. She could still taste his mouth on hers.

If she had known he was all but engaged to Christa, would she have pushed him away? With all her heart she wished she could say yes, but she was far from certain. Even now, knowing the truth, she ached to feel his arms around her again, his searching mouth commanding hers while their bodies entwined in ecstasy.

She wanted more, she realised in dismay. She wanted a lifetime with Bryan as her partner and helpmate. The truth dawned on her with shocking force. She wanted his love, and it was not for her.

Stop it, she told her thoughts angrily. With David, she could give the excuse of ignorance. With Bryan, there was no such justification. The way her mind insisted on fantasising about him was mortifying. Maybe he was right and her moral standards were suspect after all.

'Do you love Christa?' she asked, her voice coming out low and tremulous. It was none of her business, but she felt driven to ask the question.

'I'm going to marry her.' He didn't seem to notice that it wasn't an answer.

She fiddled with the buttons on the Chesterfield. 'Is it because her father expects it?'

Again he slammed the window-frame with his open palm. 'I expect it, damn it. Christa and I are a good team. When she was little more than a kid she worked alongside her father and me to help save Bowan Run. She seems to know what I want almost before I want it.'

The irony of this wasn't lost on Jill. Christa had recognised the attraction between her and Bryan from the moment Jill arrived. Her veiled warnings had been designed to impress on Jill the importance of the status quo. It seemed she was right.

Her throat dried and she swallowed hard. 'Then why did you kiss me just now?'

His eyes blazed and a muscle worked in his jaw. 'Can't you work it out?'

'I'd still like to hear it from you,' she whispered. How could he think she had a stage-managed some kind of seduction scene just to get her own back on him for bringing her here against her will?

'Then here it is. I kissed you because I have never wanted to hold a woman so much in my life. I wanted you badly, Jill. I still do. But I'm not going to give you the satisfaction of another scalp for your belt, least of all mine.'

The question was torn from her. 'But how can you think of marrying Christa when you say you want me? Surely that isn't fair to her?' Or to me, she thought angrily. His accusations cut her to the quick, so unfair and totally wrong were they.

'I'm sure you have Christa's best interests at heart,' he sneered. 'But we've managed without your touching concern and I'm sure we'll continue to do so, long after you go back to where you belong.'

'Are you sure Christa will always want to stay here?'

His features darkened, a frown etching deep into his forehead. 'This is plan B, is it? Try to undermine the relationship by letting me know about Christa's restless streak. I'm well aware of how she feels, so you're wasting your time. She's young. I wouldn't expect her to want to settle down just yet.'

'But when you're ready you'll expect her to be,' she surmised, frustrated that he always seemed to be one step ahead of her, even to understanding exactly what drove Christa.

'Of course; not that it's any of your business.'

Kissing her had made it her business, she thought in an agony of despair. Somehow she had allowed him to slip under her guard. No, there was no *allowing*. She could no more have turned aside the tide of passion flowing between them than she could stop time passing. It was so unfair that it had to end this way. 'Then there's only one thing for me to do,' she said dully.

His lip curled into a sneer. 'What might that be?'

'Go back to Perth as soon as possible.'

Lightning shards of anger pierced his midnight pupils. She almost expected to see sparks flying from them as he said, 'Now we get to the point. Do you make a habit of using your sexuality as a bargaining chip to get what you want?'

Her eyes flew wide. 'No! It isn't like that. I simply thought——'

'You simply thought all you had to do was bat your big, beautiful eyes at me and I'd melt, doing your bidding without a second thought. Well, it won't work. You heard Fred today. He's counting on the tourism project, and you aren't going to let him down.'

'Can't you see that we'd be playing with fire?'

'You might be. I've had plenty of experience at fire-fighting. I should think today's demonstration was ample proof that I can handle any fire you care to light.'

But could she handle her own feelings? The strength of her response to his lovemaking had shaken her far more than she was willing to let him see. Was this part of her punishment—to endure being near him, knowing how he was capable of arousing her, yet be unable to control any part of the situation? How could she possibly endure a month of this torment and still be expected to produce anything worth while?

Pride stiffened her spine. He might know the effect he had on her—Lord knew, she was only too well aware of it—but she didn't have to admit it. If she did, there was no way she could finish the project with her self-respect intact, and she wasn't about to give him any more satisfaction than she had to. There was one other option. She could let him think his suspicions about her motives were justified.

'You men flatter yourselves,' she said in a deliberately light-hearted tone. 'You said you want me, but you didn't ask how I feel about you.'

He rested both hands on the back of the sofa, his face looming alarmingly close. His breath was soft wind against her cheek. 'Go ahead. This should be fascinating.'

She smiled a calculating little smile. 'You're right; it was a game. But not to get my own way. I wanted to find out how it felt to be seduced by a "ten" on my Richter scale. I'm thinking of writing a follow-up article about you for the magazine.'

'If you should live long enough.' His fingers flexed as if he imagined them curved around her slender neck. 'I'd be furious if I thought there was a grain of truth in that outrageous statement. This was no research project. You weren't faking a thing when I kissed you.'

She affected a shrug. 'Who said I was faking? There's no law against enjoying one's work, is there? I suppose you're annoyed because I'm not devastated about you and Christa.'

'Liar,' he said smoothly, his mouth creasing into a taunting smile. His hand slid around the nape of her neck, teasing the tiny hairs to alertness until a shiver slid down her spine. 'One touch is all it takes to prove the effect I can have on you any time I choose.'

'You bastard. If this isn't sexual harassment, I don't know what you'd call it.'

His eyes darkened persuasively. 'I'd call it out-and-out seduction, except that I have no intention of taking it a step further than it suits me.'

She leapt from the sofa and crossed the room to stand near the window, hoping the shadows would conceal how badly she was trembling. Damn it, she still wanted him, knowing that his touch was calculated to have exactly this effect on her. 'I could tell Christa what you've said,' she threatened with little conviction.

'She'd find it highly amusing,' he returned, unperturbed by her threat. 'Especially as she knows what I think of you.'

Her mouth tightened into a bitter line. 'Of course, she so helpfully showed you my column, didn't she?'

'It's the kind of loyalty I expect from anyone close to me.'

It was hardly loyalty when Jill knew that Christa hoped to change Bryan's mind about remaining here, but there was no point in saying it now. He was in no mood to listen to anything she had to say. He was enjoying himself far too much, watching her squirm.

How long could this go on? He was determined to have her stay, even though everything which had happened between them urged her to leave as quickly as possible. 'How can we possibly share the same roof on a purely business basis after today?' she asked, changing tack.

'I see no difficulty whatsoever.'

'Because you can separate bedroom and boardroom without a problem,' she hazarded, not surprised when he nodded comfortably. 'Well, I can't.'

'There's no other way.'

'Yes, there is. I can finish the job from Perth. My media contacts are there anyway, so it's a logical solution.'

'Except for one thing. You need a feel for this area which you can't get by fax or telephone.'

Her heart sank as she realised he was right. 'Surely there isn't much more I need to see?' she appealed.

Couldn't he see that she had offered the only workable solution? Perhaps he could contain the attraction sizzling between them, but she wasn't so sure about herself.

At least back in Perth she wouldn't have to stare into the unbelievable blackness of his eyes, seeing herself reflected there in tiny perfection. His cleft chin would be beyond her reach, the sculpted dark hair a teasing memory. Most of all, his wide, full mouth with the jutting lower lip wouldn't be able to inflame her beyond endurance, promising pleasure she had no right even to imagine.

'The crater,' he said at last, breaking into her tortured thoughts. 'You've seen most of the stock route, so all that remains is the meteorite crater at Turuga.'

She kept her face carefully expressionless. Perhaps once she'd seen the crater he would be willing to let her leave and complete the project from Perth. 'Could one of your men take me there tomorrow?'

'No, they couldn't.' His crisp denial cut across her question.

'You wouldn't...' she began on a rush of suspicion.

His eyebrows arched devilishly. 'Why wouldn't I take you to see the crater myself?'

'Because you and I...we'd...'

'We'd what?' he asked with maddening coolness.

She felt her face flood with colour. Alone in the desert, it would be all too easy for the chemistry between them to flare afresh, swamping all the reasons why it was impossible to give in to it. Bryan was enjoying toying with her as if she were a fish on a line, she could see, but what if his iron control eventually snapped? It was madness even to consider it.

Anger rose in her, overcoming all her injunctions about not provoking him. Who did he think he was, playing with her like this? 'We'd probably get on each other's nerves,' she said, striving to match his cool tone.

'I can handle it,' he said, mocking laughter glinting in his eyes. 'Can you?'

'You're enjoying this, aren't you?' she threw at him, wishing she had a heavier weapon than words. Something large and heavy and very breakable.

He folded his arms across his chest. 'Oh, yes. It's a better retribution than I'd hoped for.'

The sound of a car crunching on the gravel driveway caught her attention. She never thought she'd be glad to hear the sound of Christa's car, but she was.

'Christa's back,' she said warningly. Surely he wouldn't continue to taunt her after the other woman joined them?

What bound him to Christa? He didn't speak of her like a man in love. Was it passion they shared? The thought filled Jill with savage anger, until she wondered why it mattered to her. They were welcome to each other.

By the time Christa joined them in the library, Bryan had crossed the room and was pouring himself a drink from the well-stocked bar. The last few incandescent minutes might never have happened. 'Drink?' he asked Jill.

She shook her head. 'No, thank you.'

'I'd love one. Gin and tonic, please,' Christa asked, catching Bryan's question as she breezed into the room. She threw herself on to a chair and fanned her face with one hand. 'It was a hot drive out to the Run and back. The breeding programme is right on target,' she said to Bryan.

When he handed her an ice-encrusted glass, she smiled her thanks, making Jill's stomach turn over. Watching them together made something shrivel inside her, although she hated to examine too closely what it might be.

'What have you two been doing all afternoon?' Christa asked after a long draught of her drink.

Jill was thankful that she had refused a drink. She would have choked on the answer to Christa's question, betraying herself completely. But Bryan was unperturbed. 'We were discussing the cattle drive. Jill's going to finish developing the project from her office in Perth.'

Christa's eyes gleamed. 'That's wonderful news. I mean about your plans, of course. When do you intend to return to the city?'

She might have at least pretended regret, Jill thought with a pang. But it was too obvious that she couldn't wait to have Bryan to herself again. 'Bryan wants me to take a look at the Turuga crater so I can incorporate it into the plans,' she admitted.

She had the satisfaction of seeing Christa's face fall. 'Surely it isn't necessary to go to Turuga? It's only a massive hole in the ground, and overgrown as well, isn't it, Bryan?'

'Perhaps, but I feel it's important for Jill to see it for herself. I shall drive her over there tomorrow.'

Christa looked dismayed. 'But I was counting on you coming with me to Dad's place tomorrow. I'm in charge of a charity fund-raiser, and it would be great if you'd agree to be the auctioneer. You know we always raise more money when you mastermind things.'

'I'll have Mac Doohan handle it for you,' he stated.

She looked unhappy. 'Mac's no substitute for you, darling.'

'I'm sure he'll cope.'

'But there's all the setting up to be done.'

'You can take Sharkey Wilson with you. I won't need him at the Run until the weekend.'

Aware of Bryan's growing impatience, Jill leaned forward. 'If you're short-handed, I can go back without seeing the crater.'

Christa flashed her a triumphant look. 'There, you see? Jill's perfectly happy to give the crater a miss.'

'I've no doubt she is,' he said evenly. 'In the interests of being helpful, I'm sure.' The warning look in his eyes told her she wasn't getting off so lightly.

'But I want to take some spare parts over to Turuga tomorrow, so it suits me to drive there.'

Just as it suited him to test her endurance to the limits, Jill was sure. He had no more wish to play tour guide to her than she had to accompany him, but this was a sweet way of getting his revenge, and he wasn't about to waste it.

'I suppose if you go, Jill can leave by the end of the week,' Christa said petulantly.

Jill wished there was another alternative, but she could think of none, even if Bryan would allow it. After today's experience, spending a day alone with him at the crater wasn't just playing with fire; it was pure madness, but what choice did she have?

CHAPTER EIGHT

NEXT morning a stranger waited in the driver's seat of the jeep to take her to Turuga. He had Bryan's strong features and athletic build, but there the resemblance ended.

When she climbed in beside him, his greeting was coolly impersonal. He'd behaved more warmly towards acquaintances at the Royal Hotel.

She'd been dreading having to face him, but, perversely, she felt cheated by his attitude. Foolishly, she longed for some sign of the passion which had flared so incandescently between them the day before.

She tried to tell herself it was for the best. She hardly saw the outskirts of the town sliding by. Her thoughts kept returning to the man at the wheel, although she was sure he hadn't spent last night lying awake, thinking of her, as she'd thought of him. She'd tried every relaxation exercise she knew to invoke sleep without success. As a result, she was heavy-eyed and her head ached this morning.

For all of ten seconds, she'd debated about asking him to postpone the trip, but it would only delay her return to Perth. So she had forced herself to get up, shower, and dress in the outback uniform of jeans and cotton shirt with a shady hat jammed on her dark brown hair. Her skin glistened with a protective film of sunscreen lotion.

'You didn't eat much breakfast this morning,' he said as the road slid away beneath them.

As usual, Christa had cooked an enormous breakfast, but Jill had been unable to face it, settling for fruit and coffee instead. 'I wasn't very hungry,' she admitted. She hadn't felt this off-colour since her collapse at work.

'Fortunately I brought plenty of supplies.' He indicated a portable cooler strapped into the back of the vehicle. 'If you feel peckish, say so. There's enough in there to feed an army.'

Christa must have been up at dawn to pack the hamper and prepare a full breakfast as well as get ready for her own expedition, Jill thought a touch acidly. It was difficult to compete with such perfection.

Not that there was any competition, she admitted reluctantly. He had made his choice crystal-clear yesterday. For whatever reason, he was committed to Christa. Not even the passion which had flared between them was going to be allowed to interfere in his plans. If anything, he seemed to enjoy taunting her with what she couldn't have.

She made herself pay attention to the landscape. She would need to be able to conjure it up in her mind when she was back in the city.

The buildings were soon left behind as they travelled along a graded dirt road between rugged breakaways and eroded boulders, their colours jewel-like in the morning sun. Here and there, stands of stately desert oaks shaded the landscape, their pine-like needles spreading a soft carpet over the sandy soil.

This was ancient gorge country, Bryan pointed out with all the impartiality of a tour guide. In the dry season the creeks were reduced to freshwater pools, home to Johnson River crocodiles, fresh-water sharks and wading-birds.

There were birds everywhere, from cockatoos and cranes to crows, brolgas and whistling ducks. Bryan knew them all and identified them for her as they appeared.

The main track was well-defined if bumpy, but Jill spotted numbers of forks and side-tracks, wondering aloud where they went.

'They aren't tracks,' he informed her. 'We call them "highways to nowhere". They're seismic "shot" lines, made by grader for geological exploration.'

'They look like major highways.'

He nodded. 'Some of them run for hundreds of kilometres before they stop in the middle of no-where. The geologists used to think the tracks would simply grow over in time. But they can take years to disappear, and sometimes never do. Even experienced stockmen have lost their lives following these phantom roads.'

She shivered.

'Probably why it's called mother earth,' he said. 'She's contrary enough to be female, all right.'

It was said so softly that she wasn't sure whether it was intended for her ears, so she chose to ignore it. The same could be said of some men, she thought defiantly.

They stopped to boil the billy at a freshwater lagoon shaded by tall eucalypts. Bryan could just as easily have brought a flask of tea, but she had

to admit there was something special about boiling
water in a blackened billy can over an open fire.
He added handfuls of fragrant tea-leaves to the
simmering water, stirring it with a forked eucalypt
twig.

During the break, he seemed determined to
maintain his impersonal façade. 'Have you heard
from your brother and sister?' he asked when they
were both settled in the shade with enamel mugs
of tea and Christa's pumpkin scones.

'I called them last night on the radio telephone.'
She didn't add that it was the sight of a cosily dom-
estic Bryan and Christa which had filled her with
such loneliness that she was driven to call her
family.

He sipped his tea, his eyes dark over the rim of
the mug. 'How is Denise and the baby?'

'They're fine. The hardest thing for Denise is
taking things easy. She's normally so active, but
she has no choice. She's terrified of something
going wrong a second time.'

'What happened the first time?'

'She miscarried soon after they moved into
Wildhaven. Nick blamed himself for taking her
there, but the doctor said it could have happened
anywhere.'

'He's probably right.'

The silence grew again, punctuated by the calls
of the budgerigars and finches swooping and diving
over the water-hole. 'Denise tells me one of the big
tour companies intends to bring groups to
Wildhaven next year,' Jill offered when the silence
stretched uncomfortably.

He was enjoying this, she thought angrily, forcing her to make polite conversation as if nothing had happened between them. Now he nodded coolly. 'I'm not surprised. What Nick's doing is unique. People will travel a long way to see native animals first-hand. It's bound to succeed.'

'Which should please you,' she volunteered with a touch of asperity.

He looked surprised. 'Shouldn't it?'

'It is a valuable investment,' she observed.

He cradled the mug in both hands and regarded her steadily. 'There is a point to this, I imagine.'

Bitterness fuelled by frustration filled her. Not only could he ignore what had happened between them, but it seemed he had also dismissed from his mind the reason why she had agreed to come to Bowana in the first place. 'The point is, you did threaten to foreclose on their mortgage to coerce me into coming with you.'

His eyes narrowed as steam from the tea curled in front of his strong features. 'In business, you use whatever advantages you have.'

'Even if it involves innocent people?'

'Perhaps you should have thought of them yourself, before you created the problem in the first place.'

Resisting the urge to fling the remains of her tea over him, she kicked a tree stump instead. 'You bastard. You're enjoying every minute of this, aren't you?'

He was unmoved by her anger. 'I warned you from the start that you were taking on the wrong man.'

Her eyes blazed, but she recognised the futility
of continuing this argument. She felt dangerously
close to her emotional breaking-point. Was this
what Bryan was waiting for? Her complete and utter
capitulation?

It would come sooner than he thought if she kept
letting him provoke her. It wouldn't change anything, and, given the potentially explosive chemistry between them, it was foolhardy for her to be
other than carefully polite.

Finishing her tea, she resolved to take a leaf out
of Bryan's book and be as distant as he was, if it
killed her. Which was a distinct possibility, she
thought, as he doused the fire and buried the
remains.

With every sure-footed move he made, she was
reminded of the feel of his arms around her. The
strong hands bringing water to douse the fire had
heated her skin to fever pitch. Her senses had sizzled
like the hot coals, only to be buried under the reality of his commitment to Christa.

It was the cruellest irony that she had resisted
coming with him, and now the thought of leaving
him was tearing her apart.

When they were under way again, he gestured
around them. 'From here on, this is all McKinley
land. We drove on to Turuga Station just after the
turn-off to the billabong.'

The road was heavily corrugated and pitted with
holes filled with dust which rose in clouds as they
passed. Bryan called it bulldust.

'I can see why,' she said. The grains seemed to
seep into every crevice of the vehicle, filling the air
with chalky powder. 'What does Turuga mean?'

'It's an Aboriginal word for "falling star".'

She smiled. 'Another appropriate name, given the number of meteorites which have fallen to earth in this part of the world.'

His expression lightened fractionally, easing the tension between them. 'True enough. More than half the meteorite fragments found in Australia come from this area, including the lunar rock you held in your hand yesterday.'

His enthusiasm warmed her, and she dropped her head back unconsciously, as if to bask in it. 'What's so great about finding a chunk of the moon?' she asked in a curious tone.

Hooked, as she intended, he launched into a long discourse about the scientific importance of meteorites. 'They're our only tangible way to learn about the history of the solar system. Astronomy looks at it from a distance, but you can hold a moon rock in your hand, analyse it, and see what it can tell you about the birth of the planets.'

Hearing the laughter she tried in vain to suppress, he ground to a halt. 'I'm lecturing, I know, but space rocks are a hobby of mine. They can tell us so much about what happened beyond our own planet.'

'I don't mind, honestly,' she insisted, warmed by the sudden thawing in his attitude. If it took rocks to make him drop his icy façade and relate to her, then they would discuss rocks. 'How can you be sure your lunar rock is really a piece of the moon?'

'It contains a high concentration of a chemical component which is unique to the moon.'

'Just like the rocks brought back by the Apollo astronauts.' She remembered a press briefing she'd attended on the space programme. 'Oh, Bryan, this has got to attract visitors to Bowana. Where else can they touch a chunk of the moon and see where it landed?'

'Not to mention taking part in a real-life cattle drive over a historic stock route,' he added. 'I don't know why it didn't occur to me a lot sooner.'

'Perhaps you're too close to it to see it the way I do.'

He nodded, gripping the wheel tightly as he negotiated a corrugated stretch of road. 'I've been riding these tracks all my life. It never occurred to me that a tourist might find such everyday activities interesting.'

'That's just the point; it isn't everyday to city dwellers. To us, driving cattle over trackless spinifex plains is an adventure, a chance to get in touch with part of our past.'

She felt rather than saw his eyes switch to her, then back to the road again. 'You really believe it will work, don't you?'

'Is it so surprising?'

There was a slight pause before he said, 'Given what I know about you, yes, it is.'

'What you *think* you know, you mean.'

He read the challenge in her voice. 'There isn't much speculation involved. Your relationship with David Hockey is fact. You don't deny it, do you?'

'I deny that it was as sordid as you're implying. I truly didn't know that he was still married.'

'But you continued seeing him after you knew the truth.'

There was no question in the statement, and his clipped tone made her cringe. His investigation had been thorough. 'All right, I did see him a few times after I found out, but only because he swore he and his wife were estranged. He said it was only a matter of time before he was free. Until then, he wanted to go on seeing me discreetly.'

'And you believed him?' She couldn't blame him for sounding sceptical. With hindsight, she wondered herself how she could have been so naïve. She had believed what she wanted to believe.

'It hardly matters now, does it?' It was true, she found to her satisfaction. David no longer mattered to her. She could think of him without emotion, as part of her past. She'd come a long way since arriving at Bowana.

Or was it Bryan's influence? Perhaps the discovery that he could desire her so strongly had restored her self-esteem. Even though there was no future in it, she had the satisfaction of knowing it was true.

'Stop the car, please,' she appealed suddenly.

The jeep lurched to a juddering stop. 'What's the matter?'

She pushed her way out and barely made it to the roadside before spasms of sickness gripped her. She was dimly aware of Bryan holding her until they passed, then he fetched her a tumbler of water from the cooler. 'What brought that on?'

White and shaking, she sipped the water. 'I don't know. It hit me suddenly, without warning.'

'Do you often get car sick?'

'Never. It must be something I ate.'

He frowned in annoyance. 'You ate almost nothing this morning and we both ate Christa's scones, so they're in the clear.'

Trust him to defend the other woman's cooking, Jill thought with bitter irony. She was fairly sure she knew what was the matter. Yesterday's experience had left her stomach tied in knots, a feeling she recalled only too well from her recent illness. Added to a sleepless night, it was a wonder she was functioning at all.

She debated whether to ask him to take her back to town, then decided that the sooner she got the background information she needed, the sooner she could leave altogether. Only then could she truly relax.

Forcing a smile, she handed him the glass. 'I'm fine now. Whatever it was has passed off.'

'Are you sure? I planned to deliver some spare parts to Turuga Homestead this morning, but they can wait if you want to go back to town.'

'You needn't change your plans on my account,' she insisted, hating to have him witness her momentary weakness.

'Since I've already changed a good many of my plans on your account, one more occasion hardly matters,' he pointed out, controlled anger vibrant in his voice. He was probably furious with her for not being able to keep pace with him.

'I told you I'm perfectly willing to go back to Perth.'

'Ah, yes, you'd like that, wouldn't you? It would get you off the hook. But it isn't going to work.'

His comment stung her to anger. 'I suppose you think I got sick so you'd have to send me back.'

He reined in his temper with an obvious effort. 'I wouldn't put it past your devious mind, although I doubt if you're that good an actress.'

'Maybe I was yesterday.'

His hand grazed her cheek, the slight contact burning like a brand. 'Oh, no, you weren't acting then any more than you are now.'

Damn him. He knew how he affected her and he wasn't above exploiting it for his own ends. For a moment, she wished she *were* unwell enough to be taken back to town. Being out here with him and unable to do anything about her wayward feelings was the most exquisite torture she'd ever experienced.

It was the last conversation they had for many kilometres. Bryan drove in silence, seeming to welcome the ruggedness of the road. She guessed it gave him something to fight against as he wrestled the wheel over the endless corrugations.

After her bout of sickness, Jill felt empty and cold, but blamed some of it on his hostility. Why couldn't he give just a little, instead of keeping up this relentless vendetta against her?

They arrived at Turuga Homestead well before lunchtime, and Bryan disappeared into an enormous shed to hand over the spare parts. Instructed to wait for him by the car, Jill defied him by taking a walk around the area.

It was her first visit to a large outback property as an adult. As a child, she'd attended barbecues where whole trees were felled across creeks to provide the fire, and had spent time in shearing sheds, helping to trample the wool down into the bales with the other children. Now she was amazed at how different everything looked.

As a small child, she'd treated it all as a huge game. Now she saw it for what it was: a lifelong struggle against the elements for simple survival. This was emphasised by the huge water tanks dwarfing the main house. In the background, generators hummed, a further reminder that nothing could be taken for granted in the outback.

The homestead was more like a small town than a single dwelling. Around the main house were clustered dwellings for station staff as well as cattle and machinery sheds. In between were the weathered railings of the stockyards. In one yard a group of dusty-looking cattle huddled in the sparse shade of a gum tree.

She leaned against a railing and pushed her hat back off her forehead to mop her damp brow. How could she have hated the outback so much when she was a teenager? Then she had only seen the loneliness and the despair. Watching a young calf nuzzle its mother, she smiled. There was hope here, too, and redemption in winning the struggle against nature.

'Couldn't stay put, could you?'

She started as Bryan materialised behind her. The soft dust had muffled the sound of his boots.

'I'm not a child to be ordered around by you. If you must know, I was revising a few memories.'

'From your childhood?' he surmised correctly.

'Yes. When I was younger, all this seemed so dusty and horrible. I couldn't wait to escape to the city.'

'It is dusty and horrible at times.'

She hated to admit it, especially to him. 'But it's exciting, as well. It's ... it's real.'

He surprised her by nodding agreement. 'Out here, what you have counts for less than what you are. It's a different world.'

And a lot of good it did her to realise it now, she thought angrily. This world belonged to Bryan and Christa, not to her. 'We'd better get to that crater of yours,' she said, and headed for the jeep.

'How far is it from here?' she asked when they were under way again. This time they didn't take any obvious road, but bumped and rattled across a paddock. Several times Jill had to jump out and open stock gates, then close them again after Bryan had driven through.

'It's only another few kilometres.'

'Thank goodness.' The work of opening and closing the gates had exhausted her. The afternoon heat beat down on the jeep relentlessly, defying the car's cooling system. Her headache had worsened, and every bump and jolt of the vehicle was magnified through her body.

He gave her a sidelong look. 'Your love-affair with the outback was short-lived.'

Her body was damp with perspiration, but she had to force the words out through parched lips. 'I didn't realise how far the crater would be.'

'It isn't far in outback terms. But it's almost over now.'

Almost over. The words pierced the cotton wool which enveloped her thoughts. Her stay at Bowana was almost over. The visit to the crater was the last piece of the puzzle. There was no more reason for her to remain here. Even if she had wanted to stay, it wouldn't work. How could she remain around

Bryan, knowing the effect he had on her, when there was no possible future in it?

'What did you say?'

'I said we've arrived.' Bryan's words penetrated her foggy mind, but it was an effort to get out of the car. When had her limbs become so leaden?

His intense gaze raked her. 'Are you all right?'

'It's probably just the heat,' she insisted, not wanting him to think she was looking for sympathy.

He offered her a drink of water from the cooler and she drank it greedily, holding out the cup for a refill almost immediately. When the second disappeared almost as quickly, Bryan insisted that she rest in the shade before they explored the crater.

Her legs seemed to fold under her so she collapsed to the ground rather than sitting down. Perhaps she should have insisted on going on while her strength held out. Resting with her back against a tree, she wasn't sure she'd be able to get up again.

She made a determined effort to concentrate. 'Tell me about the crater.'

'It equals the third largest in the world, the second being Wolfe Creek to the north of here,' he explained. 'Turuga wasn't discovered until the early 1950s, although it was probably known to the locals before then.'

Forcing her eyes to focus, she took in the circular rim which began not far from their feet. They were sitting on the sloping outer wall, which rose higher than a building above the surrounding sand plain. Trees and shrubs covered the floor of the crater itself.

All around them were huge spheres coloured with the local iron oxide. 'What are they?' she asked, indicating the nearest of the spheres.

'They're called shale balls, thought to have been piled here when the meteor landed,' he explained. 'Some of them weigh a couple of hundred kilograms.'

'Bigger than your average football,' she murmured.

'The Aboriginals have their own explanation for the crater,' he went on. 'They say it's the place where the rainbow serpent emerged from the earth, the shale balls being her eggs.'

His voice seemed to recede from her like the tide as his words became a meaningless jumble. Distantly she heard the enamel mug clatter over the shale as it slipped from her fingers. She tried to force herself to her feet, shaking her head to drive away the encroaching fog.

'Jill, what is it?'

'I . . . I feel terrible.' The ground lurched beneath her and she grasped the nearest support, which happened to be Bryan's arm. It closed around her, steadying her, as she willed herself not to disgrace herself by fainting at his feet.

She'd bet that Christa had never fainted in her life. The thought rallied her meagre resources enough to straighten up, although Bryan kept his arm around her waist. It felt oddly comforting.

'I'll help you back to the car.'

He supported her stumbling progress back to the jeep, where he cleared the back seat and forced her to lie down. As she lay with her eyes closed, he soaked a cloth in water and placed it across her forehead. The coolness was blissful.

Moments later she heard him fiddling with the two-way radio, and struggled upright. 'What are you doing?'

'I'm contacting the flying doctor. You need help.'

She shook her head. 'Please don't; they'll only tell me what I already know.'

He paled under his tan and grasped her wrist in a grip of iron. 'What's the matter with you?'

Shaken by the intensity of his concern, she managed a tremulous smile. She would have given a lot to think that his concern meant he cared about her, but she knew better. 'It's nothing serious. I caught a stupid virus that laid me off work for a while. I was warned that it takes a while to get completely out of your system.'

His expression hardened. 'Why the hell didn't you tell me you'd been ill?'

She pressed the compress against her forehead, the coolness reviving her a little. 'My doctor said I was over the worst. All I have to do is get some rest and avoid stress.' Which was hardly what she'd been doing.

He looked angry enough to break her in two. His fingers flexed as if he could barely keep his hands off her, and not for any purpose she'd welcome. 'You are without doubt the most stupid female I've ever met.'

In her weakened state, his attack was enough to bring tears to her eyes. 'Now listen——' she began in a choked voice.

His hands clasped her shoulders and he hauled her close. 'No, *you* listen. You may think that life is a game, but out here it's precious.'

'Even my life?' she asked, doubting it where he was concerned.

The expression in his eyes was unreadable. 'Oddly enough, it is,' he said, sounding strained. 'It isn't something I expect you to understand. You're too busy being Superwoman.'

CHAPTER NINE

JILL had never felt less like Superwoman as she endured the trip back to Bowana. For most of the journey she floated in a twilight world between sleep and wakefulness, hardly aware of her surroundings. When Bryan insisted on leaving the jeep at Turuga Homestead and flying back to town in a light plane belonging to the station, she protested weakly about not wanting to be a nuisance, but he over-ruled her.

'For once you'll do as you're told.'

He was furiously angry, and it was beyond her confused state to work out why. She'd only tried to do what he wanted. Why was he so annoyed with her?

When she heard him radio ahead and ask for someone to meet the plane, she knew better than to object. This was yet another facet of Bryan McKinley, a grim-faced, take-charge man who looked as if he would kill anyone who stood in his way.

Even so, she drew the line at using the wheelchair which an attendant wheeled up to the plane. She allowed Bryan to help her on to the tarmac, but stood her ground when he tried to steer her any further.

'I'm all right, honestly. I'd rather walk.'

The attendant directed a questioning look at Bryan, who dismissed him with a nod of his head and a murmured thank-you. Shrugging, the man wheeled the chair back inside the single-roomed terminal.

'You will let Dr Brennan take a look at you.' It wasn't a question. She sensed she'd have a fight on her hands if she refused.

'All right, but he'll only confirm what I've told you. I've been overdoing things a bit.'

'A bit?' His anger exploded in the two words. 'Spending hours in the library researching then insisting on trekking all over the bush is hardly "a bit".'

A shaky smile trembled on her lips. 'All right, maybe it was too much, but I enjoyed myself. I didn't realise it was taking such a toll.'

He led her to a station wagon parked in the car park, probably also conjured up while they were in the air. She collapsed into the front seat thankfully. It had taken all her remaining strength to walk from the plane to the car.

Driving towards town, he glanced at her white face. 'Why didn't you tell me you were on sick leave when I found you at Wildhaven?'

'I didn't want you to think I was evading my responsibilities. I wasn't looking for sympathy.'

His grip tightened on the steering-wheel. 'Of course not; you wouldn't know what to do with it. I think you had another reason for keeping the truth from me.'

She looked away. It wouldn't be hard for him to work out why she had agreed to come. His threat to foreclose on her brother's mortgage had been the catalyst, but she couldn't deny the powerful attraction she'd felt for him at that first meeting. He had drawn her irresistibly. Did he suspect how she felt?

'You knew I'd find out the truth eventually,' he went on. 'No doubt you thought it would be fun to make even more of a pest of yourself than the column had already done.'

This was the last thing she expected. Hurt, she retorted, 'How? By ruining my own health?'

His mouth tightened into a grim line. 'It does seem illogical even for you. So why didn't you tell me?'

Closing her eyes, she let her head drop back against the leather head-rest. 'I didn't think you'd believe me.'

'Am I such a tyrant?'

She kept her eyes shut. 'No, but you were furious with me for writing the column. I was sure you'd think I was malingering if I told you why I was on leave.'

'I probably would have,' he agreed, his voice hard. 'But surely your doctor in Perth would have backed you up?'

'I wasn't thinking too clearly at the time. Besides, the job you wanted me to do didn't seem too stressful.'

Neither had it been until the attraction between them had flared into passion. The job was stress of a different kind, and she could have coped with it. Finding out that he considered himself engaged to Christa had done more damage, she accepted.

They completed the short journey in silence. The doctor was waiting when they arrived at Bryan's house, and frowned when he saw her on her feet.

'You're not related to Bryan, by any chance?'

Her puzzled look flickered to him, then back to the doctor. 'No, why?'

'I wondered if your stubbornness is genetic.'

Bryan's refusal to leave them alone while the doctor checked her over added weight to the doctor's theory. He compromised by letting Bryan wait on the veranda outside the French windows while he completed his examination.

'I tried to tell Bryan it was a stupid virus,' she said when the doctor pulled his stethoscope away from his ears.

'You're taking this far too lightly,' he cautioned, wagging a finger at her. 'Unless you look after yourself, you leave yourself wide open to further illness. Surely you own doctor made that clear?'

She gave a shuddering sigh. 'She did—quite graphically, in fact. Taking a holiday in the country was her idea.'

'I'm sure she didn't have sunburn and heat exhaustion in mind.'

Jill gave a weak laugh. 'Her prescription was more like "plenty of rest and no stress".'

When Dr Brennan began to prepare a syringe she pulled a face, but let him administer the vitamin injection he advised. Anything which helped her get back on her admittedly wobbly feet was welcome right now, and she said so.

It was Dr Brennan's turn to frown at this notion. 'You're going nowhere for the time being, young lady. Unless it's to a hospital if you don't co-operate. I'm prescribing at least a week of R and R with no stress or exertion of any kind.'

Collapsing against the pillow, she watched the doctor repack his bag. When he had gone, she viewed her situation with dismay. Given Bryan's contempt for her, he would be furious to have her inflicted on him for a week, when she could do no useful work on the project.

When he returned after seeing the doctor out, his expression was as unyielding as granite. His eyes were dark with barely restrained anger.

'What the hell do you think you were doing, roaming around the outback when you were less than fit?'

It was on the tip of her tongue to remind him that he had insisted on taking her to see the crater, but that would be begging the question. Why hadn't she told him that she was still recovering from the effects of a virus? Was it because he already made her feel so ridiculously feminine and vulnerable that she hated to add to the feeling?

'I thought I was fit. I'm sure this is only a passing thing. I'll be fine by tomorrow.'

His mouth tightened into a grim line, and steel glinted in his sardonic gaze. 'Not according to Dr Brennan. It seems you're to stay put for at least a week.'

A week when she couldn't be of any use to him, except as an unwanted responsibility. 'At least I can continue my research while resting,' she volunteered, her eyes flashing a challenge which he met with unwavering ferocity.

'No.'

It was said with such brutal finality that she felt driven to respond. 'That's it, Bryan? Just a flat no?'

'You heard me. The doctor's orders are to rest, and rest is what you will do.'

'If it kills me,' she muttered savagely. It was fairly clear that he intended her to make as speedy a recovery as possible, the sooner to be rid of her.

'If the virus doesn't, I may,' he responded to her muttered comment. 'You are without doubt the most intractable female I've ever had the misfortune to encounter.'

Her head came up. 'Because I wrote the truth about you in my column?'

'Because you care so little for your own well-being.' He loomed menacingly over her until she wondered if he meant to shake her, but it was only to adjust her pillows. 'At least the doctor's vitamins have put some colour into your cheeks,' he observed tautly.

It was more probably caused by his nearness, she thought. At his glancing touch, the blood began to pound in her veins and her sensitised skin was flooded with prickles of exquisite awareness.

Unwillingly, she recognised that her foolishness in keeping her convalescent state from him had put him at risk, too. He looked drawn after the long drive and the mercy flight, although the light of battle lit his dark eyes. Fine lines radiated out from his eyes and deepened to valleys on either side of his mouth. Smoothing them away with her fingers was a disturbing temptation. With an effort, she kept her hands on the bedclothes.

Before she could say or do anything else to incur his displeasure, Christa burst into the room. 'I met the doctor outside the house. What's this about Jill collapsing at Turuga?'

'It's nothing, really,' Jill insisted.

Bryan's eyes narrowed. 'Nothing but the after-effects of a serious illness which require her to rest here for at least a week.'

A look of dismay coloured Christa's delicate features. 'A week? But Jenny's getting married in four days. We promised to be there.'

'You promised, not me,' he said, sounding as if they'd had this discussion before. 'Jenny is an old friend of Christa's,' he explained for Jill's benefit.

'Then you must go. I'll be fine by myself,' Jill insisted.

Christa grimaced. 'The wedding is in Perth.'

'Oh, dear.'

'Indeed. So you can see why it's not convenient to have an invalid on my hands this week.'

'Jill is not an invalid, and I thought I was the one being inconvenienced,' Bryan intervened. 'It is my house, after all.'

'Of course, dear. I forgot my place for a moment. It won't happen again.' With a fierce look which belied her meek words, Christa flounced out of the room.

Jill threw back the bedcovers.

Bryan was beside her in an instant, forcing her back on to the bed. 'What do you think you're doing?'

'Getting up. I can't let my stupid weakness come between you two.'

Effortlessly he grasped both her wrists in one hand and pinned them to the pillow over her head. 'Let's get one thing straight. You're a guest in my house, and neither Christa nor anyone else has a thing to say about it, understood?'

His iron grip made a mockery of her feeble struggles. 'It's understood, you . . . you tyrant,' she ground out through clenched jaws.

He gave a satisfied nod. 'Much better.'

'Now will you let me go?'

'When I'm ready.' Without releasing her hands, he bent his head and pressed a kiss against her lightly parted lips. Desire knifed through the deepest realms of her being as his chest hair grazed her skin where the buttons of her shirt gaped open from the doctor's ministrations. Before she could react to the kiss, he straightened and freed her hands. 'Now I'm ready.'

'Why did you do that?'

He shrugged. 'Despite what you wrote in your column, I make no claim to sainthood. If you could see how you looked just now, you'd know why.'

Before she could summon an answer he turned away, his stockman's boots clicking on the polished wooden floor as he slammed out of the room.

For a long time she lay unmoving, her hands clasped over her head, her thoughts in turmoil. Was he trying to remind her of her place? He made no secret of wanting her, yet he had no intention of giving in to it. Was his kiss meant to demonstrate the strength of his resistance to her?

'Damn, damn, damn,' she muttered. Why couldn't she be as blasé about this as he was? Why did she have to ache for his touch with every fibre of her being?

She should be scrubbing his kiss off her lips in disgust. Instead, she savoured the taste of him like a teenage fan who'd been brushed by her favourite pop star. 'A Bryan groupie, that's what you are,' she told herself in annoyance.

Well, it would have to stop. She had no choice about remaining here until the doctor cleared her to travel, but she could choose how she responded to Bryan's presence. At least she hoped she could.

Worn out by her ordeal and the effort of jousting with Bryan, she slept heavily, not stirring until well into the evening when Christa came in with a tray.

'Good, you're awake,' she said. 'Bryan gave orders not to disturb you until you woke of your own accord.'

Feeling like a fraud, Jill sat up so the other woman could settle a tray across her knees. She hadn't realised she was hungry until the aroma of cheese omelette and herbed vegetables teased her appetite into life. 'You shouldn't wait on me; you have enough to do,' she said apologetically.

Christa sniffed. 'True enough, but Bryan has other ideas. I must admit, this was a clever move.'

With a forkful of omelette poised in mid-air, Jill froze. 'I beg your pardon?'

'You must have realised he's a sucker for anything lame. Nothing else could have gotten him on your side so effectively.'

'You're wrong,' Jill denied, shocked by Christa's reasoning. 'I really am on leave because of the virus. Today's reaction wasn't part of any scheme.'

Scepticism clouded Christa's features. 'Have it your way, but you may as well accept that Bryan and I have an understanding. This isn't going to change anything.'

'I know. He told me.'

The frank admission caught Christa by surprise. 'He did? Then ... you really are ill?'

'Yes, so you can stop worrying about me. Bryan's incredibly loyal.' And besides, he hates me, she added inwardly.

Red tinged Christa's cheeks, but Jill couldn't decide whether it was with embarrassment at her mistake, or with a lover's pride. 'He is, isn't he? When he promised my father we'd make a match of it, I knew he'd never go back on his word.'

'Until I came along.' Guilt suffused Jill as she thought of her own longing to feel his arms around her.

Christa twisted a tea-towel between her hands. 'I could see he was attracted to you. I should have had more faith in him, shouldn't I?'

'Maybe now you will.'

Christa moved away. At the door she turned, her manner hesitant. 'He will come to love me, you know, even though he's marrying me because he owes my father such a lot.'

Jill was at a loss. She had assumed as much, but was astonished to hear Christa spell it out. 'Your father must be a remarkable man to inspire such devotion,' she dissembled.

Christa's face fell. 'He was, once. Since his stroke, he's a shadow of his old self. I think he's only clinging to life to see Bryan and me married.'

A hissing breath escaped Jill's lips. So Christa's father was dying. No wonder Bryan felt bound to her. He was too much a man of honour to break a promise, especially to a man who had done so much for him and now wanted only one thing in return before he died.

A sense of hopelessness overtook her and she pushed the tray away, the food barely touched. 'I've had enough, thank you.'

Christa heard her defeated whisper and removed the tray. 'I thought you might. Pleasant dreams now.'

Her dreams would be anything but pleasant, and Christa probably knew it. Morning seemed like an eternity away.

For the next two days, Jill discovered what it was like to be well and truly pampered. Perhaps as a result of their discussion, Christa looked after her with good grace, plying her with magnificent meals and waiting on her hand and foot.

'You're spoiling me,' she protested. 'I don't need morning and afternoon tea as well as lunch. I'll end up as big as a house.'

'I'll bet when you're at home you live on those frozen diet meals,' Christa said.

It was close to the truth. 'In that case, I'll enjoy this while it lasts,' she said, helping herself to a scone, still warm from the oven.

Christa pulled a chair up beside her on the veranda and poured herself a cup of tea. 'Bryan's gone to visit Dad and he'll probably stay for dinner, so I can take it easy this afternoon.'

Jill had felt his absence as acutely as she felt his presence these days, but she kept her thoughts to herself. Now that she and Christa had reached an understanding it was pointless to stir up more trouble.

She flicked crumbs off the rug draped over her legs. 'When are you off to your friend's wedding?'

'Tomorrow. I'll be back in a couple of days.'

'Perhaps I should go with you.'

'Bryan won't hear of it until the doctor clears you to travel,' Christa confided.

Jill knew why. He wanted her to complete her assignment without further mishap. All the same, a slight glow of satisfaction crept over Jill. She was foolishly pleased that he had vetoed her departure. For all the good it would do her, she thought in annoyance. Daydreaming was becoming a bad habit lately, especially since most of her fantasies revolved around a certain unattainable man.

Christa looked pensive as she stirred sugar into her tea. 'Is there anyone you'd like me to contact for you while I'm in Perth?'

Jill shook her head. 'Thanks, but no. I've written to my parents to let them know where I am, and I'll telephone Nick and Denise again later. There's no one else.'

There was a sudden flare of interest in Christa's eyes. 'Not even David Hockey?'

Jill's head snapped up. How did Christa know about David, unless Bryan had confided in her? Annoyance bristled through her. How dared he discuss her personal life with Christa? 'What makes you think he'd be interested in my welfare?' she asked, her tone brittle.

Some of the other woman's saccharine warmth vanished abruptly. 'There's no need to play coy, Jill. I know you and he were an item. I suppose you thought you'd be better off finding yourself a wealthy grazier.'

Jill sucked in a sharp breath. Was Christa relaying what Bryan himself believed? 'I didn't want to *find* anyone,' she denied furiously. 'As it happens, David is married.'

Christa's eyes flew wide. 'Really? Your journalistic sources did let you down, didn't they?'

'In David's case, yes, although I wasn't exactly thinking along those lines when I met him.'

'How romantic. Was it love at first sight?'

Thinking of her reactions around Bryan, Jill doubted if love was the right word for what she'd felt about David. She'd never felt the throbbing need to touch and be touched by him, nor ached to feel his arms around her, his mouth fiery against hers. Nor had he ignited her temper to the same degree that Bryan did.

'It was probably more interest at first sight,' she answered Christa's question belatedly. 'We were covering the same story and went for coffee afterwards. It grew from there.'

Christa sighed deeply. 'What fascinating circles you move in. I feel like a real country mouse by comparison, although I'm sure Bryan prefers not to have to compete for my attention.'

There was no answer to this, since Bryan had made his feelings quite clear. Draining her cup, Christa stood up. 'I'd better finish packing. You can use the library if you want to telephone your family.'

Reminded of Christa's place as mistress of the house, Jill suppressed a surge of resentment. What else did she expect? That Bryan would keep her confidences about David to himself? She was furious that he had shared them with Christa. How else would she have come by the information?

Denise's voice on the phone was a welcome diversion. Her sister-in-law had wanted to come and take care of Jill until she managed to talk her out of it.

'You must think of the baby,' she urged. Reluctantly Denise had agreed, but only on condition that Jill kept her posted about her recovery, especially hearing that Christa was to be away as well.

'Don't worry, I can take care of myself,' Jill assured her.

Her words were to prove prophetic. While Christa was away, she saw Bryan only first thing in the morning before he drove out to one or other of his properties, and last thing at night when he bade her a terse goodnight as he barricaded himself in his study. She might as well have been alone in the house.

On the day before Christa's expected return he went to see Bill Bernard, telling Jill to expect him back some time in the afternoon.

'Don't do me any favours,' she muttered mutinously as he left. The day stretched emptily ahead.

Without conscious thought, she found herself in the library, poring over old records of the Bowana stock route. Reaching for a pen, she began to make notes, and was soon completely absorbed.

Lunchtime came and went. It was only when the library door slammed open that she looked up, startled to find Bryan framed there, his expression grim. 'What the hell do you think you're doing?'

He looked as if she'd been caught stealing the family silver. 'I was bored, so I decided to do a little research.'

In two strides he reached the desk and lifted the heavy book from her hands, closing it with a small explosion of sound so she jumped. 'Against the doctor's explicit orders,' he reminded her. 'Don't you ever do anything you're told to do?'

She stood up quickly, which was a mistake as her head began to swim. Instantly his hands clamped over her upper arms, steadying her. A jolt like a thunderbolt passed through her. 'It depends on who's doing the telling,' she said shakily.

His heavy-lidded gaze bored into her relentlessly. 'Obedience can be taught, Jill.'

Defiance brought her chin up, to be instantly re-gretted as she encountered his intense scrutiny. She wished now she'd taken time to have some lunch; then she wouldn't have this light-headed sensation, as if she were floating in his hold. 'Obedience implies a master, and I have no need of any such thing,' she denied.

His eyes became hooded and a faint flush seared his skin, probably from his tightly leashed anger with her. To her consternation, he freed one hand long enough to graze the side of her face with his knuckles. 'There's more than one kind of mastery,' he reminded her.

How could she deny a truth she recognised in her soul, even if her spirit didn't want to know it? 'No,' she whispered, closing her eyes against the torment of his nearness.

'No?' The question came out lazily taunting. To prove his point, he traced a finger down the side of her face, all the way across her collarbone and down to the cleft between her breasts. Under his fingers, her heart raced a frantic tattoo which must tell him how invasive she found his touch. He was waiting for her to beg him to stop, but she swallowed the words, refusing to give him the satisfaction of her surrender.

It took every ounce of control she possessed to endure his mouth wandering over the sensitive skin of her throat without crying out—not to have him stop, but to go on and on to the ultimate conclusion.

Without conscious awareness, she had thrust her head back, closing her eyes and parting her lips instinctively, so that when he kissed her her senses reeled and she had to cling to him to remain on her feet. As her nails dug into his back, she told herself it was for support, not in response to the maddening onslaught of his kisses.

He was proving his point far more effectively than even he knew, she realised. This was no more than a demonstration of his mastery over her actions. He couldn't know that he was also taking control of her very soul.

Angry resentment curled through her and she tried to push him away, her fingers sliding uselessly over the hard muscular structure of his shoulders. She wasn't going to be manipulated by him. She had been the pawn of one married man already. She wasn't about to dance to Bryan's tune, however sweetly seductive the music, knowing he was promised to Christa.

When he lifted his head, his eyes were coolly appraising. 'As I said, obedience can be taught.'

Twisting in his grasp, she shook her head. 'Not by you. You'll never control me.'

His laughter mocked her as he traced the bruised line of her lips with one taunting finger. 'Brave words, considering that I just did.'

The telephone shrilled, drowning out the denial she recognised as bravado. With a lingering look at her, he went to answer it. As she tried to leave, his hand clamped around her wrist, forcing her to stand beside him impotently as he chatted easily with a caller who could only be Christa. Hanging up, he confirmed it, adding that the other woman would be returning the next day. 'She has a surprise for you,' he said.

Another shock? Jill wondered. It could hardly compare with the one she'd just received at Bryan's hands.

CHAPTER TEN

FOR the next twenty-four hours Jill was careful to act the role of model patient, giving Bryan no excuse to demonstrate his mastery over her further.

She was almost grateful for Christa's return as a buffer between herself and Bryan. She had forgotten about Christa's promised surprise.

Christa looked lovely, with a new hairstyle and smart new trouser-suit. She was bubbling over with excitement as she dumped her suitcase in the hall and threw herself into Bryan's arms. A savage sensation erupted through Jill at the sight, but she kept her face impassive as Christa looked expectantly towards the door.

Around it stepped a tall, fair-haired man, and Jill felt her knees start to buckle. With an effort, she steadied herself, aware of Bryan's gimlet gaze on her. All the same, she felt herself go white with shock. She wanted to run, but there was nowhere she could go. She was trapped. 'David,' she murmured weakly.

He seemed impervious to the tension holding her in thrall. 'Hello, Jill. Christa brought me your message. I had to come.'

Hearing Bryan's sharply indrawn breath, Jill wanted to cry out that it was a lie, she'd sent no such message. But Christa linked her arm in Bryan's. 'Let's leave these two alone. I have so much I want to tell you.'

'Bryan, wait.'

He brushed aside the hand Jill placed on his arm and strode out of the hall without a backward glance, leaving Christa to follow hurriedly in his wake.

Tiredly Jill turned to David. 'I didn't send any message, David, and I think you know it.'

He gave her a thoughtful look. 'Maybe I did suspect your friend Christa of stretching the truth a little. But I really was concerned about you.'

'Especially after she told you about the Turuga crater,' she hazarded. The David Hockey she knew, pity help her, wouldn't come all this way out of concern for her, unless there was something in it for him as well.

He spread his fingers apart at shoulder height. 'You have to admit, it's a potentially interesting story.'

She sighed heavily, still in shock at his unexpected arrival. 'It's a good story,' she conceded. 'And these people really need the tourist interest it could generate.'

'It's as good as done. Now how about a decent welcome? It *is* good to see you again.'

'Oh, David, it would be great if you can help the town, but it's too late for us, no matter what Christa told you.'

'Are you quite sure, Jill?'

If she'd had any doubts when they parted, she was sure now. Being held in Bryan's arms was all it had taken to convince her there was no other man in the world for her. 'I'm certain,' she said, her voice cracking a little.

'If you change your mind...'

'I won't,' she said with heavy finality.

'Then I'll have to concentrate on the story, won't I?' His voice lifted a little, and she knew that he was already shrugging off any residual pain much more easily than she had been able to do. He went on to tell her about a glossy magazine which had jumped at the chance to 'discover' the crater. He was officially in town on assignment for them. 'So you see, I didn't waste any time getting my white knight act together. Surely I deserve some thanks for that, if only for old times' sake.'

'Very well, I am grateful,' she acknowledged.

'Grateful enough for a hug, as a friend?' he added hastily, opening his arms in invitation. When she hesitated, he pulled her into them and brushed her hairline with his lips. He stopped when he felt her stiffen in rejection. 'Hey, it was only a friendly hug.'

'I know, but——'

Before she could free herself, Bryan chose that moment to come back into the house. His face was set as he caught sight of her in David's arms. She pulled herself free and began to describe David's plans to publicise the town.

Bryan's eyes probed her with frighteningly cold disdain. 'Congratulations, you've achieved your aim.' There was no warmth in the admission.

Bewilderment blurred her vision. 'My aim? I thought it's what you wanted.'

It was like talking to a man of stone. 'It is, naturally. Not that you've done badly out of it yourself.'

'There's nothing in this for me.'

His look scorched her, then swept on to David like a bushfire, laying waste to everything in its path. 'Isn't there?' was all he said before storming into his study.

Stunned, she stood her ground until David nudged her elbow. 'What was that all about?'

Her hand went to her mouth. 'I don't know.' But she was afraid she did. Bryan thought that the project had brought her and David back together. It wasn't true, but why should he care anyway, when there was no room for her in his life?

David wasn't a journalist for nothing. 'I think my presence has something to do with it, and not because of the story.' He turned towards the door. 'My gear's in Christa's car. She's dropping me off at the hotel, then bringing me out to the picnic races tomorrow. It should be a good place to get some local colour. Will I see you there?'

'Probably. I don't know.' She sounded distracted. Bryan had mentioned it, but she didn't know if the doctor would sanction her going. She was desperate to go to Bryan and clear the air about David.

'Then I'll see you at the race-track.'

'All right, fine.' Anything to get him on his way so she could speak to Bryan.

When the door closed behind David, she slumped against it, feeling drained. Why was it so important to make Bryan understand the truth about her and David? She only knew that it was.

She didn't bother to knock on his study door. He was working at his computer when she came in. His back was to her and he seemed to slump over the screen. 'Bryan, we need to talk,' she said softly.

He didn't turn around. 'What about?'

She steeled herself. 'It isn't how it looks. David and I are——'

'Just good friends, I know.'

'Then why are you so angry?'

He spun around, his face so ravaged that she gasped. 'Because you deserve better.'

Why should he care? 'It doesn't matter; he's married anyway,' she reminded him.

'Divorced.'

Her eyes widened. 'What did you say?'

'On her trip to Europe, his wife found herself an Italian count. She came back long enough to divorce Hockey, then high-tailed it back to Naples, so Christa informs me.'

It was poetic justice, and she couldn't help the smile which teased the corners of her mouth. How David must hate being the one discarded. Given his attitude towards women, it wasn't before time.

Bryan misread her smile. 'So you see, the coast is clear for you now. If you'll excuse me, I have work to do.'

He turned back to his computer. Dismissed, she had little option but to leave him alone. Her thoughts churned. No doubt it suited Bryan to pair her off with David. There were fewer loose ends. But he was totally wrong. David's divorce didn't alter her conviction that he was the wrong man for her. His new status wouldn't change anything.

Bryan worked in his study for the rest of the day. Christa smugly informed Jill that David would be joining them at the picnic races tomorrow.

'You are coming?' she asked when Jill demurred.

'The doctor didn't object when I asked him, but I'm not sure. I don't really know anyone.'

Christa swept aside her objections. 'Nonsense. Bryan and I will be there, and Fred and his wife from the hotel. And, of course, your David.'

'He isn't my David. He's here on assignment, nothing more,' she answered more sharply than she intended. Christa's behaviour was getting on her nerves.

'All right, don't bite my head off,' Christa protested. 'What else am I to think when he drops everything and rushes to your side?'

'That he scents a good story,' Jill said, then dropped the subject. Protesting was only strengthening Christa's determination to get them back together. 'How was the wedding in Perth?' she asked instead.

As if she had pushed a button, Christa launched into a dress-by-dress account of her friend's wedding and her own shopping spree in the city afterwards.

'Speaking of clothes, what does one wear to a picnic race day?' she asked.

Christa thought for a moment. 'You'll see everything from big city fashions to casual clothes.' She made a face. 'The men don't bother, though. They turn up in their working clothes.'

'Who attends the races?'

'Practically everyone within a thousand-mile radius. Last year a couple came from Melbourne. The local politicians have their photos taken with the stockmen, and the bookmakers come from as far away as Sydney.'

David was right about the local colour. 'Does the McKinley Pastoral Company breed some of the racehorses?'

Christa laughed. 'All the owners enter horses and they all want to make the best showing possible, but breeding hardly comes into it. The jockeys are mostly station hands riding their own mounts.'

'I have a lot to learn,' Jill admitted. And not only about how picnic races were run.

The next day dawned hot and clear. The race-track itself was a few miles from Turuga Homestead. Bryan was to drive them there, picking up David from the hotel on the way.

Christa contrived to have Jill sit in the back seat with David, which added to the tension in the car. Even Christa's bright chatter was hard put to it to dispel the chill in the air.

To lift her flagging spirits, Jill had dressed in a smart pair of stone-coloured bermuda shorts and white cotton T-shirt with matching linen pinafore over the top. A pale straw hat and Hermes scarf completed her outfit. As she got into the car she was conscious of Christa's scrutiny, but there was no reaction from Bryan.

The only reaction she noted was a tightening of his mouth when David wolf-whistled his appreci-ation. 'I'd forgotten what great legs you have,' he said as he settled himself beside her.

Christa looked cool and feminine in a floral dress with wide shoulder ruffle, drop waist and shirred full skirt. The pastel wildflower design flattered her blonde colouring.

'My legs could stand some admiration,' she said pointedly to Bryan at the wheel.

He kept his eyes on the road. It was left to David to say, 'I noticed them, Christa, and you two will be the best-looking fillies at the track.'

Their arrival at the race-track was heralded by flocks of hawks and wedge-tail eagles circling the canvas settlement spread for some distance round the track. The only permanent structures were the yards and fences, a bar and a ramshackle building where food and drink were being set up alongside a windmill and water tank. There was also a demountable amenities block, a bookmakers' ring and judges' box.

Beside the race-track, a paddock doubled as an airfield for the day. By the time they arrived it was crammed with light planes and groups of horses.

Jill sniffed the fragrance of the drying grass. The brilliance of the light, the endless blue canopy above and the boundless plains around them stirred something deep inside her. She was in love with more than Bryan McKinley, she realised with a shock. During her short stay at Bowana, she'd fallen in love with his wide brown land.

As if drawn on an invisible string, she turned to look at him. He was casually dressed in a pale blue shirt, open at the throat, with the sleeves rolled up above muscular forearms. Narrow-legged moleskins were held up by a carved leather belt, and he wore the inevitable elastic-sided stockmen's boots and broad-brimmed Akubra. Her breath tangled in her throat. He looked as much at home as the eagles wheeling overhead.

And just as inaccessible.

She made a determined effort to enjoy the day, and was surprised by the number of locals who greeted her as an old friend. There was no shortage of men willing to show her how to bet on the sometimes chaotic events on the card.

When at last she wearied of the races, she retired to the corrugated iron shed where meals were served in a seemingly endless stream. Tonight, she was told, it would be dressed with streamers and balloons for a dance which would continue throughout the night.

Someone brought her a cold shandy and she sipped it appreciatively as she watched the action swirling around her.

David had landed on his feet, she noted acerbically. Trust him to find one of the moneyed young women partying with joyful enthusiasm. She was probably a station owner's daughter, and from the way she was laughing up into David's eyes she would be his willing partner for the night's festivities.

Mentally she superimposed herself and Bryan over the couple. What wouldn't she give to make it so?

'Why so sad? Oh, I see.' In one breath Bryan had asked and answered his own question as he followed her gaze to David and the woman in his arms. 'It's a shame you had to see them.'

'As you pointed out, David's a free agent. He can date whom he pleases.'

'He could at least be discreet about it, damn him.'

The ferocity in Bryan's voice shook her. 'I'm not involved with David, so it doesn't matter,' she said with as much dignity as she could muster. If it didn't suit Bryan because he preferred to think she was David's, then that was just too bad.

Her eyes smarted as she looked away. 'I'm going to watch the next race. Dr Brennan helped me to place a bet on the Turuga entry,' she said, putting her glass down.

First she had to do something about her stinging eyes. It wasn't because Bryan's insistence on pairing her with David had upset her, she told herself. It was the vast amount of dust being churned up by the races. Nothing more.

She slipped into the makeshift ladies' room and splashed tepid water on to her face. A voice floated through the thin corrugated iron walls. It was Christa, talking to someone outside.

'What does Suzie Mitchelmore think she's doing with David Hockey? He's supposed to be with that Jill Richter.'

At the sound of her own name, Jill's interest sharpened involuntarily. She heard another woman's voice murmuring a reply, then Christa's impatient rejoinder.

'I don't know what's wonderful about it. He's supposed to take that interfering bitch back to Perth with him. How was I to know he'd really want to write about a dusty old crater?'

So much for Christa's helping hand, Jill thought ruefully. It sounded as if her scheme had back-fired. She should let them know they were overhead, but Jill couldn't help waiting a few more seconds.

'You can have all the tourists you want, once I've convinced Bryan there's no future here,' Christa went on. 'I thought it was in the bag after I sent that awful column to his partners overseas and pointed out a few other home truths to them.'

There was a nervous giggle. 'You sent it to them? I heard the project was on hold. Imagine you being behind it. If Bryan finds out, he'll kill you.'

'He isn't going to find out, is he? But now I'm back where I started from. He still thinks this hell-hole has a future, and there's no way he'll take me away from here as long as his plans are going ahead.'

The room tilted crazily around Jill. Christa was the one who had sent the damning column to Bryan's overseas partners. What other mischief had she used to make them pull out of the deal?

She sounded pleased about her role. Didn't she see the damage she was doing, not only to Bryan, but to the townsfolk, who were desperate to establish a future for their children?

Now she understood why Christa had brought David back with her. He was supposed to carry Jill herself back to Perth out of Christa's way.

A small smile of satisfaction turned up the corners of her mouth. Christa hadn't expected David to be so enthusiastic about the crater. He was supposed to see it as Christa did—as an uninteresting hole in the ground in the middle of nowhere.

He had also thwarted Christa's plans by flirting with every woman at the races *except* Jill.

This thought caused Jill not the slightest regret. She was well and truly over David, able to work with him, although she was well aware of his flaws.

If only she could get over Bryan so easily. But he dominated her thoughts in a way David had never done. Her senses ran riot at the very thought of him, until she ached for his touch, the sensation dragging at her like a physical pain.

With an effort, she marshalled her thoughts. Now wasn't the time to think of herself. She had to alert Bryan before any more of his plans were sabotaged.

Would he listen to her? She had no proof beyond what she'd overheard. It was hardly evidence.

David.

Colour flooded her cheeks as she went in search of him. He was chatting to the station owner's daughter, their heads close together. With a muttered 'Excuse me', Jill took David's arm and towed him away to a private corner.

'Hey, I was making progress there,' he protested.

'Sorry, I need to talk to you. Was Christa enthusiastic about the crater story when she first came to you?'

He scratched his head. 'She said you had a story for me, but in her opinion there wasn't much to it, so I suppose she wasn't.'

'Would you tell Bryan that?'

'If you want me to. What's all this about?'

'I'll tell you soon. Good luck with your lady friend.' She gave him a playful push on his way.

When she turned around, Bryan was watching her from across the shed, his expression thunderous.

Pushing her way through the throng, she reached his side. 'We have to talk.'

'Settling for second best?' he drawled.

Momentarily confused, she shook her head. 'What?'

He gestured to where David was once more engrossed with the grazier's daughter. 'Couldn't tempt your friend away from Suzie, could you?'

'I didn't even try. This is more important. It's about the tourism project,' she said impatiently.

'Let's go outside.'

The races were over and a small army of volunteers were filling pens with cattle and horses for the rodeo events.

Bryan steered her behind the catering shed, away from the crowd. There was no escaping the noise and dust.

'Now what's this all about?'

She took a deep breath. 'By accident, I found out who sent my column to your overseas partners. It wasn't the only damaging material she sent them.'

His eyes glinted warningly. 'She?'

'I overheard her telling a friend about it just now. Oh, Bryan, I'm sorry but it was Christa.'

Bryan folded his arms across his chest, his expression grim. 'Was it now? How convenient for you.'

The unexpectedness of his response stunned her. 'I don't understand. Why should it be convenient for me?'

'You've lost Hockey. You can't have me as long as Christa stands in your way.'

He thought...oh, lord, he thought this was a scheme to come between them. Disappointment as sharp as a knife cut through Jill. What a low opinion he had of her, to believe she would stoop to such a lie. 'How can you think such a thing?' she asked, her voice reedy with the tears which threatened to burst through at any moment.

'I've seen you breaking your heart over your old flame. When I surprised you watching him earlier, the look on your face would have melted stone.'

His lips tightened into a thin line of disapproval. 'But I won't have you using Christa to get your own back.'

Anger exploded through her mind until she wanted to throw herself at him and rake his handsome features with her long nails. Instead she clasped her hands under her opposite arms, pressing tightly to hold in her pain and frustration. The words she was so good at using in her job deserted her. She stood mute, trembling with reaction, as he regarded her with lazy insolence.

'Are you lost for words now I've nipped your little scheme in the bud?'

Her head came up and she felt her eyes brim, blinking hard. She would *not* give him the satisfaction of reducing her to tears when the toughest of editors had failed. 'There's no scheme,' she said carefully. 'I was trying to help you.'

'By slandering an innocent woman?' His dark gaze raked her. 'I expected better of you, although God knows why I should, after the way you treated me in print.'

The tears fled, leaving her eyes gritty and aching. She forced her lips into a cynical smile. 'I didn't libel you at all in my column. It was all true. Especially the part about being a dictator. For all I know, you are over-rated as a lover as well.'

She had gone too far, she saw the instant his face changed. Determination blazed in his dark eyes and a muscle worked in his jaw as he moved with the speed of a panther to close the distance between them.

Corralling her against the shed wall, he claimed her mouth with such ferocity that she could barely breathe. His tongue thrust inside her mouth, demanding and receiving a response she was powerless to withhold. Held tightly against him, she felt her senses reel until she could hardly assimilate the barrage of sensation he forced upon her. Crushed against his chest wall, her breasts felt exquisitely sensitised, their peaks pearl-like. Where his hips pinned her against the wall, she felt a flaring of desire so overwhelming that her knees would have buckled if he had permitted her room to fall.

If not for the sudden, desperate reminder to herself of who and what he was, her surrender might have been complete. Somehow she managed to utter a faint denial.

'No?' he echoed in a drawling parody. 'Maybe next time you'll get your facts right before you resort to insults.'

Without a backward glance, he rejoined the crowd, his rejection so total that she felt numb.

If he had made love to her on the spot she couldn't have felt more devastated. Her slur against his manhood had provoked him, she knew, but nothing had prepared her for her own uninhibited response. He had wanted her to regret her reckless attack, and it had worked far more effectively than even he knew. How could she doubt his skill as a lover now? He had made her eat her words in a way which left her feeling shaky and weak at the very memory.

It galled her to think of how much she wanted him, how much she loved him, when he refused to believe her about Christa. Without trust there was nothing. And nothing was what she had with Bryan McKinley, all she would ever have.

Unable to endure the gaiety of the picnic races a moment longer, she begged a lift from one of the caterers who was returning to town to replenish the beer supply. A taciturn outback man, he didn't ask why she was returning early, for which she was grateful.

The town was deserted, the festivities continuing until well into the evening. She knew exactly what she had to do. The month wasn't up, but after today she doubted whether Bryan would care if she stayed. She would finish the project from Perth, giving him no excuse to foreclose on her brother's mortgage, but she would do it with as much distance between them as was humanly possible.

If she drove until nightfall, then slept in the car until dawn, she could be at Wildhaven by breakfast, she decided. Should she call Nick and Denise and tell them to expect her? She decided against it in case they tried to talk her out of it.

Her car was fuelled and ready, one of Bryan's men having serviced it only days before. She loaded her cases into the car, tying them down securely, and borrowed some food and water from the kitchen. Leaving money and a brief note in their place, she got into her car.

This wasn't how she wanted to leave, she thought as a bleak wind of despair swept through her soul. She had fallen in love with Bryan, and what was her reward?

Her lips retained the imprint of his kiss, and whisker burns abraded her cheeks. But the greatest damage was to her heart, which felt like a stone inside her. Unconsciously she kneaded her chest with one hand, trying unsuccessfully to banish the ache, as she drove slowly out of town.

CHAPTER ELEVEN

THERE was little time to appreciate the raw beauty of the spinifex plains. All Jill's concentration was needed both to manhandle the car along the corrugated track and to remember the way.

Time and again her mind returned to her last conversation with Bryan out at Turuga. Why couldn't he believe her? It wasn't as if she wanted to blacken Christa in his eyes.

Didn't she? a small voice whispered inside her. Wouldn't it simplify matters if Bryan was free? Was that what she had hoped to gain by confronting him.

'No,' she said aloud after searching her conscience. She knew how much the town's future meant to him. She couldn't stand by and see his dream destroyed.

It was pointless anyway. No matter what he found out about Christa, there was still her father, to whom Bryan owed so much. How could Jill hope to compete with such a powerful debt of honour?

She welcomed the solitude of the dune country. Apart from the flocks of birds in the white gums and patches of mulga alongside the track, there was peace. At sunset she would see dingoes, plains turkeys, emus and kangaroos, but for now the plains were empty of animal life.

Into the great silence she drove for hours, stopping only to slake her thirst with cool water from her supply, and to remove the clumps of prickly spinifex which clogged the radiator.

The sand around her began to glow blood-red with the coming of evening, and she stopped, looking for a place to camp. Trying to drive after dark was foolhardy. Apart from the risk of getting lost, she could run into a kangaroo and have a serious accident. Who would know or care out here?

As if in response to her thoughts, she heard the murmur of an engine in the distance. No tell-tale dust cloud marred the track either ahead or behind her. The sound came closer.

She looked up as a small white plane with blue markings on the tail came in low, following the road.

Bryan?

Wind rushed past her as he flew overhead. It was the Cessna in which they'd flown from Turuga to Bowana. She was sure she could make out Bryan at the controls. What was he doing here?

Joy spiralled through her, out of control. He had come looking for her, unable to let her go out of his life for good.

The noise became deafening as he skimmed the plane over the road then banked and turned, this time coming in to land. He had been checking the condition of the road, she realised.

He taxied the plane to a halt a few metres ahead of her car. A smile of pure happiness lit her features as he jumped down from a door beneath the high wing of the plane.

Her joy was short-lived. He looked furious as he strode towards her, kicking up dust with his boots.

'What the hell do you think you're doing?'

Her smile died. 'I'm driving to Wildhaven.'

'Not by night you're not.'

'Of course not. I intend to camp by the roadside until dawn.'

He gave her a look of grudging respect before his features hardened again. 'You probably would, too, even though it's insane to travel alone in these conditions.'

Wounded pride made her defensive. 'It's really none of your concern.'

'You came here as my guest. That makes it my concern.'

A tight band wound itself around her heart and squeezed, making her feel faint. 'Your duty towards me was discharged this afternoon. You didn't have to come all this way merely to apologise.'

His jaw tightened, the hard line emphasised by a swath of five o'clock shadow. 'I'm glad you think so, because I don't plan to apologise.'

'Then why did you come?'

'After you ran off, I got a radio telephone call from your brother. Your sister-in-law has gone into premature labour.'

Horror raced through her and she started to spin away, but his grasp on her arms arrested her. 'Let me go! I have to go to her; she needs me,' she gasped out, twisting helplessly in his hold.

He hauled her closer. 'Listen to me. You can't drive through the night in this country. You'll kill yourself.'

She turned brimming eyes to him. 'But Denise... The baby...'

'I'll take you in the plane.'

Slowly, sanity overrode her shock. 'Why should you?'

'Do you really have to ask?'

Of course. The comradeship of the outback. He was simply helping out a neighbour in her time of need. Abruptly her resistance collapsed. Denise and the baby were more important than Jill's reluctance to share the cramped confines of his plane. Her heart raced as she thought of Denise. This baby was so important to her. Please, God, don't let her lose it, she prayed as she followed Bryan to the plane.

Rescuing her bag from the car, he tossed it in after her, then drove the vehicle on to the road shoulder and locked it. Moments later, they were racing along the road and into the sky, which was stained with the orange glow of evening.

Thank goodness the small plane was too noisy for comfortable conversation. After today, what could she possibly say to him? She jumped when he jogged her arm. 'Look up there.'

Above the horizon hung a gleaming white cloud like a white satin sheet flung into the sky. At miraculous speed, it was whipped into one amazing shape after another, occasionally disappearing altogether, only to reappear seconds later in a new configuration.

'Corellas. Uncrested cockatoos,' Bryan mouthed in answer to her shouted question.

As they came closer she saw that the cloud was indeed a flock of dazzling white birds, moving and spinning around the sky in joyful formation.

Watching them soar through the clouds, she realised that they didn't disappear at all. When they changed direction, they presented shadows rather than sunlit feathers to her view.

'It's amazing,' she mouthed to Bryan, gripping his arm to make her point.

The magic of the shared moment had passed. He glanced coldly at her fingers splayed cross his forearm, then reached up to flip a switch over his head, and her hand slid away.

She avoided touching him again for the rest of the flight, only too aware of how hard it would be to stop. In spite of everything that had happened, she still wanted him desperately. The desire to touch and be touched by him vibrated through her in harmony with the throbbing engine.

Was love always such a torment? She could hardly bear to think of what Denise must be going through, all for love. It seemed so cruel that such a shining ideal should always bring such suffering with it.

'What did the doctor say?' she asked Bryan above the clamour of the engine.

His fingers tightened on the controls as if they were a bull's horns. The shape was the same, she thought distractedly. 'He wasn't there,' he said. 'He was expected when your brother called me.'

'He will get there, won't he?' Wildhaven was looked after by the flying doctor service, she remembered. Her skin went cold with fear. What if the doctor didn't get there in time?

Bryan seemed to sense her growing panic. 'He'll get there.'

But when? It was dark by the time they landed at Wildhaven. Her brother's foreman, Tom Noonagar, was waiting for them in a Land Rover.

The headlights beamed across the rugged airstrip to light their way in.

Almost before the propeller had stopped spinning, Jill pushed her way out of the plane and rushed to the waiting car. 'How is Denise, Tom?'

In the dark she could only make out his big, expressive eyes. They looked moist in the light from the car headlamps. 'She's not good, missis. No sign of that doctor yet.' His glance went to the Cessna. 'I was kinda hoping it was him now.'

Bryan reached her side and she performed a sketchy introduction. The two men acknowledged each other with a nod. 'The doctor isn't here yet,' she told Bryan, the tremor in her voice betraying her panic.

He took her arm, and some of his strength seemed to flow into her. 'Don't give way now. Denise is going to need you.'

Throwing her case into the car, Tom drove them to the homestead with reckless disregard for the rough terrain or the old man kangaroos which leapt across their path. 'I gotta get back to the airstrip and wait for the doc,' he said after he dropped them off.

The mud-brick homestead was ablaze with lights and the front door stood open. Her boots clattered across the flagstone floor as she hurried through the house. 'Nick? Denise?' she called, her voice echoing hollowly back to her.

'In here.' Her brother emerged from the master bedroom. His face was grey as he hugged her quickly. He looked distraught when Bryan followed her into the house. 'I hoped you were the flying doctor.'

A strangled cry tore the night air, and Jill flinched. 'What's holding him up?' Bryan asked Nick.

'Must be plane trouble. The base can't raise them, so nobody knows when he'll get here.'

Jill's urgent gaze went to Bryan. 'Can't you go for Dr Brennan?'

He shook his head. 'No time. From the sound of things, the baby will be here before I could locate him. But there is something we can do.'

'Fly her to a hospital?'

'I could if you want your niece or nephew to be born in a Cessna.' He nodded towards the door. 'What we have to do is help deliver a baby.'

Her brother's shaken look galvanised her into action. 'Tell me what you want me to do.'

Bryan's hand gripped her shoulder. 'Go in there and comfort Denise. Where's the bathroom?'

As Nick led Bryan down the hall, Jill took a deep breath and pushed open the bedroom door. Denise was lying on her side with her knees drawn up. A satin sheen stood out on her face.

Fighting the urge to turn and run, Jill went to her sister-in-law and grasped her hand. 'Couldn't you wait to get this over with?'

Denise opened her eyes and managed a weak smile. 'Jill, thank goodness. Did you bring the doctor?'

Jill squeezed her hand. 'Don't worry; help is on the way.'

Bryan loomed over them both. His bare forearms were red from scrubbing, and a pristine white tablecloth was tied like an apron high on his chest.

He smoothed the hair away from Denise's forehead. 'How long has this been going on?'

'It feels like most of the day,' Denise gasped out between contractions which made her grip Jill's hand like a vice.

'She didn't realise she was in labour. We both had a touch of food poisoning, and we thought it was more of the same,' Nick supplied.

Watching the waves of contractions which flickered beneath the flimsy sheet, Bryan shook his head. 'You'll have more than indigestion when this night's over—like a new addition to the family.'

He sounded so calm and assured that Jill's heart swelled. Whatever their differences, he would make things all right. Denise even managed to smile.

He nodded approvingly. 'That's the spirit. You won't mind if I lend a hand, will you?'

Biting her lip, Denise shook her head. Nick took her other hand and Bryan settled himself at the end of the bed with all the aplomb of a midwife. He must have done this before, Jill thought. He radiated confidence.

He frowned in concentration as he felt with his flattened palms for the baby's position.

'Were you expecting a breech birth?' he asked in a conversational tone. Jill caught an undercurrent of concern and felt renewed stirrings of fear. She gripped Denise's hand tighter and forced herself to smile reassuringly.

'The doctor had to turn the baby once before, but it could have moved again,' Nick said with a frown.

'Looks like it, but everything's fine. We'll get you through this, Denise.'

Another contraction gripped her, and she concentrated on her breathing before giving Bryan a grateful smile. 'I'm glad you got here in time.'

Bryan winked at Denise. 'I wouldn't miss this for the world.'

To anyone else, Jill would have screamed a denial, but she felt Bryan's assurance as a living presence. He would make it all right, she would stake her life on it.

The baby was doing just that, she realised. She made herself concentrate on blotting Denise's forehead and bracing her when Bryan told her to push.

'That's the girl. Here we go,' he said comfortingly. Denise gave a last mighty effort.

A sigh of wonder slid from Jill's lips as she caught sight of the small body emerging into his hands. He swathed it in the towels he'd brought from the bathroom. The baby's head still hadn't appeared, and the concentration on his face told her this was a crucial stage. She held her breath.

Agonising moments later, Bryan held the baby on his lap and was clearing its airways with unbelievably gentle touches. The sight of the big outdoorsman cradling the tiny new-born baby brought a huge lump to her throat. She had never seen a more poignant sight. When a lusty cry rent the air, she couldn't hold back her tears.

'Congratulations, Nick and Denise,' he said softly, his voice choked. 'You have a beautiful little boy.'

Denise gave Nick a wavering smile as he leaned over to kiss his wife. 'Well done, darling.'

Jill's eyes met Bryan's, and she was unable to disguise the powerful rush of love which radiated from every part of her being. 'Thank you,' she mouthed, her eyes wet.

There was a commotion at the door, and a man in his fifties burst in. Setting a medical bag down on a chair, he cast a professional eye over the scene and nodded in recognition to Bryan. 'Practising medicine without a licence, McKinley?'

He grinned. 'Your fees always were too high, Ned.'

Letting the doctor take over, Bryan steered Jill out into the hall. 'I don't think we're needed any more.'

She gave him a teary smile. 'Will Denise and the baby be all right?'

'I'm certain of it. The baby is early, but that's not a problem these days. The doctor will fly them to the hospital, where they'll get the best of care.'

Even as he spoke, a uniformed sister pushed past them, her arms loaded with equipment from the flying doctor's plane. 'Radio conked out,' she said apologetically as she passed them.

'So that's what it was.'

'Oh, Bryan, if anything had gone wrong...' Her voice trailed off as imagination took hold.

His arm came around her shoulder until he was supporting most of her weight. 'It didn't, which is all that matters.'

Although she had no right to it, the weight of his arm around her shoulders was warm and welcome. 'Nothing went wrong, thanks to you,' she said, her voice vibrant. 'How many babies have you delivered?'

'Counting this one? One.'

Her knees buckled and she clung to him. 'But you knew exactly what to do. How did you——?'

'One human baby and countless lambs, calves and foals,' he added. 'Birth is always a miracle.'

The greatest miracle was his handling of the crisis, she thought. She had never loved him more than at this moment, nor felt the distance between them so acutely. Wearily she pushed herself upright. 'What a night.'

It was already half over. Tonight they had shared something wonderful, but it only served to remind her that it was all they could ever share. 'Denise keeps guest rooms made up at the end of the hall. You're welcome to use one,' she said stiffly.

'Thanks, I will.' He sounded equally tense and distant. 'I'll have a shower first.'

What more was there to say? 'Goodnight, then, and thanks for everything you did.'

His dark eyes became shuttered. 'You did your share. Goodnight, Jill.'

She turned away as he headed for the shower. Some time during the evening, Tom had dumped her case in her usual guest room. A bed had been made up in the room next to hers, presumably for Bryan. An overnight bag stood on it. He must have thrown some things into it before coming to find her.

Without quite knowing what she was doing, she took a half-step inside, then another. In the next moment she was unpacking the bag, carefully smoothing creases out of a checked shirt she found crammed on top. Somehow the fabric found its way to her cheek and she pressed her face into it, en-

joying the freshly laundered feel of it. Tomorrow
he would wear it next to his skin.

A vision of him cradling Denise's baby, so tiny
and fragile in his strong hands, filled her mind. She
squeezed her eyes shut as a spasm of intense longing
gripped her. Longing for what—a baby? Bryan's
baby, she thought despairingly. Seeing him holding
the new-born infant had awakened yearnings she
thought she'd left behind for good in Bowana.

'What are you doing here?'

As if stung, she dropped the shirt on to the bed
and whirled around. He had come straight from
the shower, wearing only a towel wrapped around
him like a sarong. His chest was bare and glistening
with droplets of moisture.

Her tongue darted across her parched lips. 'I
didn't... I just... I keep thinking about Denise.'

'She'll be fine. She's a bit groggy from something the doctor's given her, but she and the baby
are in the best hands. They wanted to get her to
hospital, so I said goodbye and gave her your love.'

'Good. Thanks.' She gulped as a tear rolled down
her cheek. She tried to brush past him, but he
caught and held her. When she tried to wrestle free,
his hold tightened.

'Don't fight it. It's only reaction. This has been
a traumatic night.'

'B-but it's over.' Why should she feel so
tremulous now when the worst was behind them?

'That's the best time to give way—when you've
done your part.'

He was only being kind, doing what anyone
would have done in the same circumstances, she
told herself. It didn't mean anything. But it felt so

good to have his arms around her, like a home-coming after far too long away. She gave a soft sigh. 'I can't help thinking of what could have gone wrong tonight.'

He crooked a finger under her chin and lifted her head. 'As I told you, it didn't, so relax.'

If he hadn't kissed her lightly to seal the assurance, she might have found the strength to return to her own room, but the touch of his lips was as heady as wine. Thirsty for more, she was hardly aware of tilting her head back in silent invitation. 'Oh, Bryan.' All her longing for him went into the two words.

Exactly when the embrace changed from comforting to something deeper she wasn't sure, but she felt it in the way his arms tightened around her.

It was madness, but with every sense working on overdrive she was powerless to end the embrace. She wasn't even sure she wanted to. Tonight she had seen a new life born and it had touched a chord deep inside her, a need she hadn't even known she possessed. She had also seen how fragile and precious life could be. As was love.

She opened her eyes and he read the message in them. His mouth sought hers, and there was no more comfort in the kiss. In its place was an urgency so powerful that it filled her with wonder. Excitement coursed through her as the hands which had given life to a new baby now slid across her fiery skin, his touch tender yet demanding.

Lost in the enchantment of his embrace, she threw her head back, needing him as she had never needed another human being, wanting him as she had never wanted another soul.

The baby's first cry found an echo in the sound which escaped from her own throat as he buried his face in her shoulder. 'Yes, Bryan, yes.'

Cupping his head, she let her fingers tangle in his hair. His hand slid inside her shirt and she gasped as he found her breast and massaged it, her nipple tingling as he palmed it gently but insistently.

Slowly he eased her backwards until she lay across the bed, his shirt crumpled beneath her. She tried to speak, to tell him of the wonder of this moment, but his kiss sealed her lips and she knew there was no need for words. His kiss was as sweet as wine and his arms were a safe haven she needed desperately. When he unbuttoned her shirt, she gave a cry of delight as her breasts spilled into his hands and she saw his eyes light with appreciation of her beauty.

When he took her in his mouth, she writhed in delicious torment. His towel had fallen unheeded and his body moulded against her, magnificently masculine and demanding.

Under his touch, the rest of her clothes slid away until there were no more barriers. His hard body felt hot, heavy and wonderful against her feminine softness as he came to her.

'Not quite yet,' he murmured, reaching a long arm out for his bag. 'Help me to be ready for you.'

He made the precaution a shared pleasure, she thought in wonder as he guided her hand lower. She teased him at first, drawing out the suspense until she could stand it no longer, then quickly sheathed him so there would be no more delays. Wanting him was like the most exquisite hunger, gnawing at the deepest recesses of her being.

When he satisfied the hunger at last, a soaring
sensation tore through her. His possession was as
wondrous as she had dreamed it would be, more
so for being real at last.

She clutched him, wanting him even closer,
wanting the impossible. No greater closeness could
exist anywhere. With him, she moved and breathed
as one.

The dream went on and on. An ache gathered
inside her, a wanting such as she had never experienced before. The urgent feeling tantalised her,
just out of reach. Then it was there, rolling over
her in mind-tearing waves until she felt as if she
must die of ecstasy.

His fingers gripped her shoulders as he crested
the peak with her. Slowly, slowly, she coasted down
the other side, her ragged breathing gradually returning to normal.

Only then did the enormity of what she had done
dawn on her. Swept away on an emotional tide after
the birth of the baby, she had allowed Bryan to
make love to her in spite of all the reasons why it
was wrong.

A sharp pain stabbed through her. How could
she have forgotten that he was promised to someone
else? She sat up and drew her knees up against her
chest. He slid a hand down the satiny skin of her
back. 'What is it?'

Her chin sank on to her knees. 'I didn't mean
this to happen.'

'Neither of us did. Tonight was like being in a
war zone where all the normal rules are suspended.'

Her heart sank. His meaning was all too clear.
Nothing had changed between them. This was

merely an aberration because they had both been under such tremendous pressure. Making love to her had been a safety valve, nothing more.

Stiffly she got out of bed and reached for her shirt, thrusting her arms into the sleeves mechanically. 'You could stay,' he said as he watched her.

Shaking her head, she gathered up the rest of her clothes and pulled her shirt around her like a robe. 'No, I can't.' She had already made enough mistakes for one night.

She noticed that he made no more attempts to stop her as she fled back to her own room.

CHAPTER TWELVE

THE lowing of the calves beneath her window roused Jill from sleep. Groggily she looked around. Where was she? Then the night's events came flooding back and she felt her face grow warm.

She knew what was wrong. After the emotion-charged arrival of Denise's baby, Bryan had made love to her. Thinking of the way she had gone to his room, she wanted to run and hide. How could she have behaved so recklessly? How could she face him this morning? Or herself?

'Good afternoon, sleepyhead.'

She forced a smile. 'Afternoon? What happened to morning?' she asked as her brother came in with a tray of coffee and hot buttered toast.

He grinned. 'You slept through it. I only came in because I heard you stirring.'

She sat up, pulling the covers around her. 'You should have woken me hours ago. How are Denise and the baby?'

'I rang the district hospital this morning and they're both doing well. I'll go over to see them later in the day.'

Sipping her coffee, she smiled at her brother. 'Congratulations, Daddy.'

'Congratulations yourself, Aunty. I'll bet you never expected to be part of the action.'

She grimaced. 'It's still hard to believe.'

Nick nodded soberly. 'I hate to think what would have happened if Bryan hadn't known what to do.'

This wasn't the time to tell Nick that it was Bryan's first and only experience of delivering a human baby, she thought. 'Where is he now?' she asked. She felt far from ready to face him yet.

It seemed she was worrying needlessly. Nick looked uncomfortable. 'He flew back to Bowana earlier today after getting a telephone call from someone called Christine or something.'

Her heart gave a painful lurch. It hadn't taken Bryan any time at all to fly back to the other woman's side. 'It wouldn't have been Christa, by any chance?'

'That's the name. Apparently she needed him urgently, so he dropped everything and flew home. He said to tell you he'll contact you as soon as he can.'

The toast turned to ashes in Jill's mouth and she swallowed hard. She shouldn't be surprised, but it hurt to have Nick spell out the reality. How could she have been such a fool?

'Maybe you should rest a bit longer. You've gone quite pale,' Nick said in concern.

She lifted her chin. 'I'm fine, thanks. As soon as I've finished this, I'll get up and make myself useful around the property.' At least Wildhaven needed her, even if Bryan didn't, she thought miserably.

Her brittle tone betrayed her. 'Is everything all right, sis?'

'Just reaction after last night, I expect,' she said with forced cheerfulness.

'Well, don't overdo the chores. You're still convalescing yourself, remember?'

'Yes, boss.'

He gave her a suspicious look. 'When you call me boss, I worry.' He dropped his voice. 'I gather you didn't expect Bryan to take off for Bowana this morning.'

Her eyes clouded and she focused on the coffee-cup cradled between her hands. There was no point in pretending. Nick knew her far too well. 'I should have expected it, but I guess I was hoping against hope that things would turn out differently.'

He tilted an eyebrow at her. 'This Christa wouldn't be the fly in the ointment, would she?'

She gave a heavy sigh. 'Yes, she is. He's engaged to her.'

Nick let out a sympathetic breath. 'Bad luck, sis. It's shades of David Hockey all over again, isn't it?'

'No, it isn't. This time I'm not giving up so easily.' Even as she said it, she knew it was true. Finding out that David was married, she had quietly left the scene, nursing her damaged feelings in solitude. Yet David's marriage had foundered soon afterwards through no fault of Jill's. Who knew what would have happened if she'd refused to give up?

The truth was, she hadn't fought for David because she hadn't really loved him. Bryan was different. She knew now that she loved him with all her heart and soul. She couldn't let him go so easily, not now she had known the unbearable sweetness of his possession. If Bill Bernard was half the man they all thought he was, he would want Bryan to be happy, she was sure. Maybe she could plead with

Bill Bernard to intercede on her behalf. It seemed
unlikely that he would take her side against his own
daughter, but miracles did happen. Last night was
proof.

Nick watched her warily. 'What are you scheming
about now?'

'What makes you think I'm scheming about
anything?'

'I know that look, little sister, and all I can say
is, Bryan McKinley better watch out.'

A woman scorned had nothing on a woman
loved, she thought as she shooed Nick away and
got out of bed. Her head was buzzing with plans.
As soon as Bryan telephoned, she would let him
know she was coming to Bowana.

A day later, her plans started to look foolish.
Bryan still hadn't phoned, and it was all she could
do not to try to contact him. Only the thought that
his silence was intentional held her back. She
couldn't bear it if he told her he never wanted to
see her again.

Two of Bryan's men had driven her car to
Wildhaven that morning, but had left almost immediately, before she could ask them what was
going on at Bowana.

She eyed her car thoughtfully. Tom Noonagar
could service and refuel it for her, then she could
drive north without waiting for Bryan's call.

If she wasn't welcome, she couldn't feel any worse
than she did at this moment. But at least she would
know the truth, once and for all. Bryan loved her.
She knew it as well as she knew her own name. The
only uncertainty was whether he would make a
place for her in his life.

When Nick returned from the hospital he brought the welcome news that Denise would be allowed home the next day and the baby soon afterwards. She hugged him warmly. 'That's wonderful news, Nick.' It also meant he wouldn't miss her help with the property.

Nick looked doubtful when she told him her plans. 'I'm not happy about you setting off on your own.'

She planted a sisterly kiss on his cheek. 'You don't have to be happy about it. You only have to make sure my car's in good shape.'

'It'll be in tiptop shape,' he promised. 'Will you at least take a two-way radio with you?'

At least she'd be able to contact someone if she ran into car trouble. 'Yes, I will,' she agreed. 'And thanks for caring so much.'

Her brother had the transceiver installed by lunchtime, and gave her a thorough lesson in its use, including the required frequencies for contacting the flying doctor service. 'If you get lonely you can tune into the galah session.'

She smiled. 'I haven't heard that expression since we were kids.'

It was the term used to describe a sort of openline radio session when residents of far-flung stations could chat to one another. For her, there would be no chatting on this trip. Her head was too full of plans for what she would say to Bryan when she saw him.

Nick was still trying to talk her out of going when she set off. She had ample supplies of fresh water, enough food to feed an army, as she laughingly assured him, and advice on handling every conceivable emergency.

'You didn't lecture me like this when I travelled with Bryan,' she protested.

'You were in his hands then.'

She was still in his hands, if the truth be admitted. Her entire future depended on the reception he gave her at Bowana. 'Give my love to Denise and the baby,' she told Nick as she got into the car.

'I will. Tell Bryan we're naming the baby James McKinley Richter after the man who brought him into the world. We want you two to be godparents. Do you think he'll agree?'

'After midwife, godfather should be a snap,' she said.

Before her brother could think of anything else to delay her, she gunned the motor and drove out through the gates of Wildhaven.

Nick was right: it had felt different travelling in convoy with Bryan. His presence had reassured her. She felt his absence more keenly than she would have thought possible as she navigated the first rough stretch of bush track towards the billabong where they had shared their first billy of tea together.

She bypassed the billabong and drank her tea by the roadside, under the shade of a stately desert oak. With only the birds for company and the occasional wild camel running ahead of her car to avoid the prickly spinifex grasses, she felt more alone than she had ever done before.

To pass the time as she drove she put the finishing touches to the tourist project in her head.

David's article would start the ball rolling, then other papers and magazines would follow, with television and radio coverage as well if they were lucky.

The publicity would fuel interest in the pioneer cattle drive, which would be marketed as a holiday package to tourists in Australia and overseas. If it was the success she hoped, the Bowana cattle drives would become a 'must do' for visitors to the outback.

She would more than pay her debt to Bryan for writing the damaging column, she thought with satisfaction. How different things would have been if the mistake had never occurred. She would never have met him, she thought with a pang, far less fallen in love with him.

That column had a lot to answer for.

Her attention was drawn to a stand of native white cypress trees, their artistically gnarled grey limbs fringed with green, in contrast to the earthy tones around them. Why hadn't she noticed these strikingly handsome trees on the last trip?

She hadn't noticed them because they hadn't been there, she thought with a shiver of apprehension. For the first time she noticed a track leading to the base of a small sandstone rock formation which nature had shaped and banded into folds. It was also unfamiliar.

Worriedly, she stopped the car and walked the short distance to the base of the rock formation, noting how delicate ferns grew in the crevices of the overhanging rocks. At one end of the rock formation was a cluster of Aboriginal paintings.

The designs of circles, lines and squares were faded and weathered with age, but she recognised the wavy outline of a rainbow serpent and what looked like tribal figures carrying the snake on their shoulders.

She shivered, not understanding the meaning, but instinctively recognising the spiritual importance of this place. She didn't belong here.

Back at the car she faced facts. Somehow she had turned on to one of the seismic 'shot' lines Bryan had told her about, the wide, inviting 'highways to nowhere' bulldozed out of the bush for gas and oil exploration.

The phantom highway ended not a hundred metres from where she stood. Beyond it was virgin bush.

Wearily she reached for the radio, but before she could do more than activate it a voice breached the silence. It was such a welcome voice that she almost broke down in tears.

'Bryan, is that you? Over.'

'Jill, where the hell are you?'

She almost laughed aloud. If she knew the answer she wouldn't be on the radio, calling for help. 'I don't know,' she admitted shakily. 'I turned off on to one of those exploration corridors you warned me about. It runs out not far from where I am.'

There was a moment's crackling pause, then he came back on the air. 'Give me what landmarks you can.'

In as much detail as she could, she described the track leading to the sandstone bluff and the cave paintings she'd discovered.

'It sounds as if you're at Lightning Man rock,' he explained. 'It's a sacred place where the thunder and lightning were supposedly made by the dreamtime spirits.'

'It sounds silly, but I have the strangest feeling I shouldn't be here,' she told him, clinging to the reassuring familiarity of his voice as to a lifeline.

'You shouldn't. Lightning Man is taboo to women. I wouldn't hang around if I were you.'

A shiver gripped her and her hand tightened on the transceiver. 'I don't plan to stay longer than I must, if you'll just tell me the best way out of here.'

'Do you recall seeing a windmill a few kilometres before the sandstone bluff?'

She thought for a moment. 'Yes, there was a sort of wooden fence contraption around it.'

'That's the place. Use the windmill as a landmark and drive towards it. You'll cross a dry creek and come to a large open flat. After another small rise, you'll be looking down on the windmill among a stand of melaleucas. You can camp at the well for the night, then rejoin the stock route a few kilo-metres south of there.'

Relief flooded through her. She would soon be on her way to his side. 'What did you say?' she asked as the message began to break up in static.

She thought she caught the word 'darling' before the message faded altogether. No amount of fid-dling with the radio could get him back.

It wasn't until she gave up on the radio and began to follow Bryan's directions back to the main track that it occurred to her to wonder how he'd known where to find her. He hadn't asked what she was doing here, either, she thought irritably. Maybe he didn't care.

Had she totally misread the garbled word? She didn't like to think so, but she must have done.

She followed his directions carefully until she was back at the main track. Night was falling rapidly by the time she stopped to make camp.

Too tired to think of cooking anything, she ate some sandwiches from the store Nick had provided and drank cool water from the well, then crawled into her sleeping-bag, stretched out on the back seat of the car. The loneliness closed around her and she fell asleep thinking of Bryan.

In her dreams he became confused with Lightning Man and tried to make her go away. He kept telling her she didn't belong here. It was taboo.

Taboo. Taboo. Taboo.

The words resolved themselves into insistent tapping on the window of her car. Struggling to emerge from her sleeping-bag, she realised that Bryan was outside, tapping to waken her. It was daylight outside.

It was all she could not to fling herself at him as she emerged from the car. She knew she looked tousled and grubby, yesterday's shower seemingly a long time ago. He didn't seem to notice as he swept her into his arms.

'Thank God I found you, Jill. I've been driving for most of the night, trying to locate you, after Nick radioed that you were on your way. I was about to turn back to Bowana when I finally spotted your car at the well.'

Blinking sleep from her eyes, she leaned into his embrace, revelling in the feel of his arms around her. 'What are you talking about? You knew where I was. You told me to camp here.'

He gave her a patient smile. 'Are you sure you're fully awake? I haven't spoken to you since I left Wildhaven. I wanted to call, but too much was happening.'

She shook her head as if to clear it. 'Wait a minute. You called me on the radio last night when I was lost.' Her voice faded to an uncertain whisper. 'Didn't you?'

'Where were you when the call came?'

Her throat felt parched suddenly. 'You told me . . . the call told me I was near a place called Lightning Man rock, a sacred Aboriginal site which is taboo to women.' She gave him a look of appeal. 'How would I know about it unless you told me?'

'Lightning Man rock has tremendous spiritual significance to the local Aboriginal people. They believe it's a place where dreams can be changed into reality.'

Goose-bumps sprang up on her skin and the hair lifted slightly on the back of her neck. Was there no limit to what love could do?

Had she dreamed Bryan's presence so powerfully that she had conjured him up in her mind? His voice had sounded so real, so reassuring. Yet it was possible that she had noted the landmarks herself and found her own way back to the track. The Aboriginal lore could have come from her research.

What other explanation was there?

'You are real this time, aren't you?' she asked, her voice thready with uncertainty.

His arms tightened around her. 'Can't you feel how real I am?'

Pressed close against him, she could feel every taut muscle outlined against her in graphic relief. Even to the extent of how much he wanted her. A matching desire flamed inside her, burning away the last of her doubts. 'You're real enough for me. Don't ever leave me again, please.'

His lips grazed her hairline. 'I won't, I promise. I wouldn't have left you this time if there'd been any choice.'

Yet he had gone back to Christa without a backward glance. 'It isn't enough,' she said raggedly. 'I need more from you.'

He held her at arm's length, his glittering gaze taking in every detail of her anxious expression. 'What more can I offer you?'

She understood, or thought she did. He wanted to make her his mistress. His name, his children, would be reserved for Christa.

'What we shared is much too precious to be demeaned like this,' she said in a barely audible tone.

'Demeaned?' He sounded furiously angry. 'You mean to tell me that you regard being my wife as a come-down?'

It was her turn to wallow in confusion. 'Being your wife? I don't understand.'

He gave her a bleak look. 'Bill Bernard died yesterday morning of a massive stroke.'

She was beginning to understand. She touched his cheek gently. 'I'm so sorry, Bryan. I know how much he meant to you.'

'He was like a second father to me. When I got the message at Wildhaven that he'd had another stroke, I got back to him as fast as I could. I couldn't think about anyone or anything else. It wasn't until much later that I realised how my departure might seem to you, but when I tried to call you you'd already left.

A lump rose in her throat. The message had come on behalf of Christa's father, not Christa herself. 'I thought you regretted making love to me and went back to make peace with Christa.'

'How could I, after all we'd been to each other that night? I tried to tell myself I could, but even for Bill I couldn't give you up, Jill. It was one of the things I wanted to tell him before he died. Somehow I knew he'd understand.'

She could hardly speak for the hope which welled inside her. 'Were you in time?'

'By a miracle, I was. He told me anyone who wrote all those things about me must feel something for me, so he wasn't too surprised. He was sorry about Christa, of course, but he understood. I've already told Christa.'

'How did she take it?'

He caressed her hair over and over. 'Don't worry on her account. When I told her, she couldn't wait to throw at me how she'd sent that letter to the investors. I'm sorry for doubting you, my love, but I didn't think even Christa would do anything so underhand.'

'What will she do now?'

He hesitated, as if trying to decide how to tell her. 'She's already making plans to go back to Perth with David Hockey.'

A wry smile curved Jill's mouth. 'What happened to Suzie Mitchelmore?'

Bryan's hand came under her chin and he tilted her face up to his. 'You mean you don't mind about Christa and David?'

She shook her head. 'Not any more. David will never be a one-woman man as long as there are more than two of the sex in the world.'

'It sounds as if Christa has finally met her match,' he mused. 'I wondered how you'd feel about him once you knew he was finally free.'

'By the time I knew that, I wasn't,' she said simply.

His breathing quickened. 'Neither of us was, were we, Jill? We haven't been from the moment we met.'

'Was I so transparent?'

He smiled tenderly down at her. 'You fought me like a she-devil. I was convinced you wouldn't fight so hard if you didn't feel as strongly about me as I did about you.'

Her smile faltered. 'It all seemed so hopeless. You were all but engaged to Christa . . .'

'And I had a score to settle with an upstart writer,' he finished for her.

A frown of concern creased her brow. 'Why *did* you come looking for me, Bryan?'

He slid a hand inside his shirt and pulled out a long envelope. 'To give you this.'

She made no move to take it. It looked frighteningly like a legal document. Had Bryan decided to press his case against the magazine in court after all? 'What is it?'

'Open it,' he insisted.

With fingers which trembled, she did so, then her eyes flared brightly as she saw what was inside. 'It's the title deed to Wildhaven.'

'I thought you might like to give it to Nick and Denise as a christening present.'

She could hardly take it in. 'But why?'

'I couldn't keep on holding the mortgage over a member of my own family,' he said softly.

'Your family? But they aren't——'

He kissed her lightly to silence her. 'But they will be after we're married.'

It was real, all of it. She wasn't dreaming after all. Bryan had come looking for her to take her home with him as his wife. Faint traces of moisture beaded her lashes, but they were tears of pure happiness as she nodded shyly. 'Then I'd better marry you, hadn't I?'

'For your brother's sake?'

'For mine. I love you so much.'

'And I love you, Jill Richter. More than I ever dreamed it was possible to love a woman. You're a fire in my blood.'

In a daze of happiness, she traced the outline of his mouth with her finger, drawing a deep breath as his lips closed over it. 'I thought you said you're good at putting out fires.'

His hands slid around her shoulders and he drew her tightly against him as if he never intended to let her go. 'This is one fire which will blaze for all eternity, because I intend to bank it so high that it will never, ever go out,' he promised her.

Just how he intended to bank the fires of their love, he showed her in loving detail, until whimpers of pure joy rose in her throat. No lover was more tender, more passionate, more inventive or more demanding than Bryan McKinley.

It was just as well they were getting married, she thought in the few moments of lucid thought he permitted her between each passionate assault on her senses. This sort of thing could become habit-forming.

On the carpet of desert oak needles which cushioned them, he levered himself up on one elbow. 'Do you still think I have delusions of sainthood?'

Her dreamy smile bathed him in its warmth. 'It's no delusion, my darling. To me, you are a saint.'

'Make sure you go on thinking so,' he said in mock-reproof.

'I don't think so; I know it. How else could you guide me through the desert in my dreams?'

He gave a throaty murmur of approval. 'It goes to show you what the power of love can do.'

The power of Bryan's love, she thought as she surrendered to it with all her heart. It had kept her safe last night and would keep her safe at his side for all time. How could anyone ask for more?

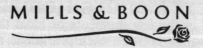

Next Month's Romances

Each month you can choose from a wide variety of romance with Mills & Boon. Below are the new titles to look out for next month, why not ask either Mills & Boon Reader Service or your Newsagent to reserve you a copy of the titles you want to buy – just tick the titles you would like and either post to Reader Service or take it to any Newsagent and ask them to order your books.

Please save me the following titles: Please tick | ✓

Title	Author	
PASSIONATE OPPONENT	Jenny Cartwright	
AN IMPOSSIBLE DREAM	Emma Darcy	
SHATTERED WEDDING	Elizabeth Duke	
A STRANGER'S KISS	Liz Fielding	
THE FURY OF LOVE	Natalie Fox	
THE LAST ILLUSION	Diana Hamilton	
DANGEROUS DESIRE	Sarah Holland	
STEPHANIE	Debbie Macomber	
BITTER MEMORIES	Margaret Mayo	
A TASTE OF PASSION	Kristy McCallum	
PHANTOM LOVER	Susan Napier	
WEDDING BELLS FOR BEATRICE	Betty Neels	
DARK VICTORY	Elizabeth Oldfield	
LOVE'S STING	Catherine Spencer	
CHASE A DREAM	Jennifer Taylor	
EDGE OF DANGER	Patricia Wilson	

If you would like to order these books in addition to your regular subscription from Mills & Boon Reader Service please send £1.90 per title to: Mills & Boon Reader Service, Freepost, P.O. Box 236, Croydon, Surrey, CR9 9EL, quote your Subscriber No:................................... (if applicable) and complete the name and address details below. Alternatively, these books are available from many local Newsagents including W H Smith, J Menzies, Martins and other paperback stockists from 8 July 1994.

Name:...

Address:...

....Post Code:..........................

To Retailer: If you would like to stock M&B books please contact your regular book/magazine wholesaler for details.

You may be mailed with offers from other reputable companies as a result of this application.
If you would rather not take advantage of these opportunities please tick box. ☐

SUMMER SPECIAL!

Four exciting new Romances for the price of three

Each Romance features British heroines and their encounters with dark and desirable Mediterranean men. *Plus, a free Elmlea recipe booklet inside every pack.*

So sit back and enjoy your sumptuous summer reading pack and indulge yourself with the free Elmlea recipe ideas.

Available July 1994   Price £5.70

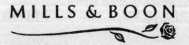

Accept 4 FREE Romances and 2 FREE gifts

FROM READER SERVICE

Here's an irresistible invitation from Mills & Boon. Please accept our offer of 4 FREE Romances, a CUDDLY TEDDY and a special MYSTERY GIFT! Then, if you choose, go on to enjoy 6 captivating Romances every month for just £1.90 each, postage and packing FREE. Plus our FREE Newsletter with author news, competitions and much more.

Send the coupon below to: Mills & Boon Reader Service, FREEPOST, PO Box 236, Croydon, Surrey CR9 9EL.

NO STAMP REQUIRED

Yes! Please rush me 4 FREE Romances and 2 FREE gifts! Please also reserve me a Reader Service subscription. If I decide to subscribe I can look forward to receiving 6 brand new Romances for just £11.40 each month, post and packing FREE. If I decide not to subscribe I shall write to you within 10 days - I can keep the free books and gifts whatever I choose. I may cancel or suspend my subscription at any time. I am over 18 years of age.

Ms/Mrs/Miss/Mr _____   EP70R

Address _____

_____

Postcode _____ Signature _____

mps
MAILING
PREFERENCE
SERVICE